THE UNFORGETTABLE
LOGAN FOSTER

by SHAWN PETERS

HARPER

An Imprint of HarperCollins*Publishers*

For Hazel and Teddy, who inspired me to write something worth reading aloud.

Library of Congress Cataloging-in-Publication Data
Names: Peters, Shawn, 1971- author.
Title: The unforgettable Logan Foster / by Shawn Peters.
Description: First edition. | New York, NY : HarperCollins, [2022] | Audience: Ages 8–12. | Audience: Grades 4–6. | Summary: Logan, an undersized twelve-year-old orphan with a photographic memory and no filter, discovers that his foster parents are superheroes in grave danger and only Logan's highly logical mind can save them.
Identifiers: LCCN 2021005540 | ISBN 978-0-06-304767-9 (hardcover) — ISBN 978-0-06-324078-0 (special edition)
Subjects: CYAC: Superheroes—Fiction. | Memory—Fiction. | Orphans—Fiction. | Foster home care—Fiction.
Classification: LCC PZ7.1.P4487 Un 2022 | DDC [Fic]—dc23
LC record available at https://lccn.loc.gov/2021005540

Typography by Corina Lupp
23 24 25 26 27 LBC 6 5 4 3 2
❖
First Edition

Hello. My name is Logan Foster. I do not know *your* name, but if you are reading this, it means I am your big brother. That is a fact.

Of course, it's possible that you are totally unaware that you even have an older brother because we haven't seen each other in more than nine years. Not since I was three and you were even younger, which would be why you don't remember me.

If you've been in orphanages or foster homes like I have been, I suppose it's possible we've unknowingly crossed paths since that time. But then there are literally billions of billions of things that are technically possible, and very few of them actually ever happen.

If you are *still reading* this, I am going to assume that you've either accepted what I've written above as a true statement, or we have met and performed a DNA test, which has confirmed my claim. Actually . . . the current, commercially available DNA test is only 99.72 percent accurate, but that still makes it significantly more reliable than just taking my word for it.

I know . . . I got off track. I do that. You should know that about me since I'm your big brother. There are probably thousands of things you should know about me. But for now, I will only list three of them since I don't want to overwhelm you.

The things you should know are:

1. I am legally named Logan Foster, which probably is not the name our parents gave me. When the security workers at Los Angeles International Airport found the three-year-old version of me in the empty Jetway of a flight that had just left for Boston, the only identification on me was a handwritten "L. Foster" on the tag of my T-shirt. The front of it read "World's Best Big Brother." I still have the shirt, even though it no longer fits.

I have been told I was given the name Logan because that is the name of the airport in Boston. I don't mind the name Logan. It's better than LAX, which is what people call the airport in Los Angeles. The last name Foster is not my favorite, even though it might be our last name. It's just not a good name for an orphan.

2. I have an eidetic memory. Most people call it a photographic memory, but most people also call spiders insects when they're actually arachnids. I can remember every detail of everything I've ever seen, read, or heard. So when I write about something someone said, that's exactly what he or she said. I have never forgotten anywhere I've been or anyone I've met . . . except for you and our parents. People call that ironic, but I think it is more frustrating than anything else.

3. I believe that you are alive somewhere and that someday I will meet you. This is not a fact, but it's also not just your standard orphan fantasy. I hear the other boys talking all the time about expecting their real parents to show up and reclaim them, just like act one, scene two of *Annie* or act one, scene six of *Les Misérables*. That's not me. I am not a little girl singing onstage about finding her parents. I am not good at singing, I am not a little girl, and I am not interested in finding our parents because they apparently were not interested in ever finding me.

However, I am very good at research, deductive reasoning, and logical problem-solving, and I intend on getting even better at all of them. So I believe I will find *you* at some point and then we will know each other. I have always believed this. But lately . . . let's just say there have been some "not normal" things going on in my life. Not that my life is ever technically "normal." But this has been a whole new level of not normal, and I've been having a hard time getting my head around it. This is rare. I generally can get my head around anything given enough time and information.

I have so much I want to tell you, and so much I want to ask you. But the way things are progressing right now . . . I decided I should probably write some of it down in case I never get the chance. You know, in case I'm dead . . . or something.

That reminds me of a fourth thing I should tell you. I don't know why I didn't include it in the top three, except that people always do things in threes, especially when they're writing. That practice goes back to Ancient Greece.

4. I'm kinda an unofficial superhero but not the kind that wears a cape or tights. So far, I have never worn tights. I have no plans to either. But I'm not sure my own plans matter much at this point.

I should probably go back to how it all started. Things start at the beginning.

That is a fact.

When I stepped into Cornwallz Comics, a brand-new shop in Santa Monica's Third Street Promenade, I was already under attack. But not from any supervillains. I don't want you to get the wrong idea. I was actually ten minutes into a relentless barrage of instructions and warnings from Ms. Kondrat, the on-site supervisor at ESTO. That stands for the El Segundo Transitional Orphanage, which is where I've lived for the past nine years. Ms. Kondrat has been there for six, even though she has quit four different times . . . three of them because of something I did or said.

Ms. Kondrat had brought me to the comics shop for an orphan's version of a bonus round with my PPs. Orphans call prospective parents PPs. It's acronymically correct, but some kids also like using the term for obvious reasons. (Say it out loud and I assume you'll get it.) So when most PPs come to an orphanage for the first round, I've observed that they kind of float around like human goldfish. They stare blankly and purse their lips until they find a kid that they think fits them—one that has the right color hair or isn't too short or doesn't eat his own boogers. That last one is what Ms. Kondrat calls a deal breaker. No one is looking for a booger eater. That is a fact.

If PPs do find an orphan they are interested in, they will launch into a whole lot of questions. These questions may include:

1. What sports do you like?
2. What's your favorite comic book?
3. What is your favorite food?
4. What do you want to be when you grow up?
5. What is your favorite subject in school?
6. Do you ever set fires for fun?

That is not an exaggeration. In the past year, I've heard three different PPs ask that last one.

If the first round goes well, and you don't tell them about any fires, the PPs may come back for a second round. This is when things start to get more serious. Usually, the couple shows up with a football or lacrosse stick or something else related to the orphan's favorite sport. But if the orphan isn't into playing sports, they will often bring comic books instead. And since I'm in the 3rd percentile for height and weight for my age and struggle to catch any type of ball, I've ended up with a decent-sized stack of comic books over the years.

I very much enjoy reading comic books. Then again, I very much enjoy reading anything I can get my hands on. But with comics, there are so many details to every frame, and cataloging superheroes' abilities is also a challenge, because sometimes the writers change them a little from issue to issue. Also, even though I only need to read a comic book once to memorize it, I keep them because at ESTO, comic books are like a currency.

You see, orphans love comic books because most superheroes are orphans. That is a fact that just about everyone knows. Superman's parents sent him to Earth before Krypton blew up. Batman's parents were shot after seeing a movie. Not only were both of Spider-Man's parents dead, Peter Parker's uncle Ben died too because Peter didn't use his powers to stop a bad guy. Most of the X-Men were orphans . . . or their parents freaked out about having mutant kids and ditched them. Even some of the brand-new superheroes whose comics books have just come out recently, like TideStrider and Quicksilver Siren, have tragic, no-parent backstories.

When I was five, one of the older boys at ESTO said that the only place you'll find more orphans than a comic book is in a Disney princess movie. That is *not a fact*. Most Disney princesses are motherless but not technically orphans. Notable exceptions include the heroines of *Frozen* and *Cinderella*. I don't know if that means that most girl orphans think they're Elsa. I haven't met many girl orphans, since ESTO is just for boys. Then again, I really haven't met many girls at all since the ones at school don't talk to me much. But I've met dozens of boy orphans in my life and they all talk about how cool it would be to become a superhero.

That was never me.

I don't really indulge in fantasies, unless you count fantasy novels, which I enjoy just as much as comic books, especially because it takes me longer to read them. I can go through a comic book in less than a minute. Given a choice, I would rather read something like Terry Pratchett's Discworld series, which is over 15,000 pages long. Of course, it's unlikely that a PP is going to bring a forty-one-book set to an orphanage, so it's just easier to say, "Yes, I like comic books."

That's what I had said during my latest second-round interaction at ESTO the week before, and that's why my most recent PPs, Gil Grant and Margie Morrow, suggested we have our bonus round get-together at Cornwallz Comics.

In preparation for the trip, I had done my research and found an article on page five of the September 2nd *L.A. Times* Westside section about all the new stores in the mall. It claimed Cornwallz had the largest selection of life-size superhero standees in Southern California.

However, I never got the chance to verify this claim because Ms. Kondrat kept demanding my attention as she went over the list of things I shouldn't say or do when Gil and Margie arrived.

You should know I am not a fan of being told what to say or do. I am even less of a fan of being told what *not* to say or do.

Ms. Kondrat had given me a list:

1. Don't ask Margie why she hadn't taken Gil's last name.
2. Don't ask why they couldn't have a child of their own.
3. Don't tell them about your eidetic memory.

The list went on, but I thought number three was strange. I know my eidetic memory is in my file. I read it one night in Ms. Kondrat's office while she was in the bathroom crying after I had shared some statistics about the odds of single women over forty getting married. The file also contained several other diagnoses, including Developmental Coordination Disorder when I was five and Autism Spectrum Disorder when I was nine. However, the only thing all the different doctors agreed about is my memory being something they've never seen before.

That's why it was also frustrating that Ms. Kondrat kept repeating her list. She knows I'm incapable of forgetting it.

Maybe she thought I was nervous because the bonus

round is the one where PPs usually will ask a kid to come live with them as a foster child. But after six unsuccessful foster placements, I no longer get nervous during the bonus round. At least, I don't think I get nervous. I'm not always so good at telling what I'm feeling. It's called alexithymia, which is the inability to identify emotions, and I assume it's why I'm even worse at telling what other people are feeling.

That said, it certainly seemed to me like Ms. Kondrat was nervous. Either that or she was coming down with a fever. Her upper lip was sweating as we waited in the air-conditioned comics shop for my PPs to arrive. To be fair, I realize it is possible that Ms. Kondrat really does have my best interests at heart. According to page four of the US Department of Health and Human Services adoption report from this year, less than 3 percent of all pre-adoptive foster kids in the country are thirteen or older. So as a twelve-year-old, this would likely be my last bonus round.

But there is another part of me, the logical part of me, that thinks Ms. Kondrat just wanted me somewhere other than ESTO. I'm not the easiest orphan she's ever had to deal with. I know this because right before Gil and Margie walked through the door, Ms. Kondrat looked me in the eye and said, "Logan, you are not the easiest orphan I've ever had to deal with. But if you can just act . . . normal . . . I have a good feeling about this for you."

Then Gil and Margie were there, smiling, and Ms.

Kondrat was smiling, but still sweating.

"Good to see you, Logan! How are you today?"

That was Margie, asking a question without breaking her smile, which I took to mean she actually wanted an answer.

"I'm curious . . . why don't you two have the same last name?"

Of course, I knew this was one of the main do–not–mention items from Ms. Kondrat's list. However, I didn't totally trust her advice, and I am also not very good at having questions in my head and not saying them out loud.

Gil answered and the words came out kinda choppy. "We only got married a few years ago . . . two years ago. And Margie has lived . . . . well, her whole life as Margie Morrow. I never asked her to . . . I mean, a maiden name isn't *made in* one day, right?"

It was a pun. I got it, but I didn't laugh. I didn't know at the time that Gil was going to keep making those jokes regardless of whether I laughed or not.

"Are you wondering because you want to know which name you might have if we . . ." That was Margie talking. She is much taller than me. She kind of hinged at the waist to look me in the eye. She also smelled a bit like warm soap. "Well, you know . . ."

I didn't know, so I said so.

"Actually, I don't know."

"I mean if we were to adopt you, Logan. Are you wondering which name you'd have?"

"Not really. I'm just curious. Also, how come you don't have children of your own?"

Out of the corner of my eye, I noticed Ms. Kondrat clench her jaw and thought I heard the sound of her teeth grinding.

Margie stood back up straighter and looked kinda sad, which even I could understand after she explained. "We've done all the tests and tried a lot of stuff I'm sure you wouldn't want to hear about . . . but the doctors told us it's impossible. Still, we think we could be good parents."

Gil nodded, like he really agreed with Margie—or maybe he was just glad he didn't have to think of a pun.

"Did you know I have an eidetic memory, which most people call a photographic memory? It freaks a lot of people out."

Gil and Margie looked at each other the way people do when they're surprised and aren't ready to be the first one to talk. Eventually, Gil gave in.

"Actually, no . . . Ms. Kondrat told us a little about the way you process things . . . but an eidetic memory, that's . . . it's something. . . . I know that's very rare. . . ."

"And special!" Margie chimed in like it was important she chime in.

I asked them a bunch of other stuff I wasn't supposed

to. Stuff about their salaries and politics and any tattoos they might have. Margie was very patient with the questions. Gil was shifting his weight from foot to foot a lot, but I figured that might be his thing. He did it a lot. Or maybe he just had to pee.

Anyway . . . I did everything I was told not to do, so I figured there was no way I was going to be fostered for a seventh time. I prepared myself to head back to ESTO with Ms. Kondrat unhappy with me, as usual.

"Logan, why don't we go outside and sit by the fountain to talk for a few more minutes, okay?" That was Margie, once again hinging to talk right at my level.

"We have something we would like to ask you." Gil put his hand on my shoulder and gestured to the door. I flinched a little when he touched me. I'm not used to being touched. I don't really like it. But I also may have flinched because I might have been shocked. Like I said, I'm not always great at telling what I'm feeling when I'm actually feeling something. Still, having been through the process before, I could see the signs. It seemed like, even after doing everything wrong, they were still going to ask me to come live with them.

However, they never got the chance to ask, and I never got a chance to decide what I was going to say.

As soon as we stepped outside, the street split open under my feet.

3:42 P.M.
FRIDAY, SEPTEMBER 17

"It's an earthquake!"

That was Ms. Kondrat stating something so obvious that I was a bit embarrassed for her.

The ground under my feet felt like it was rippling. Cracks riddled the pavement between where I was standing with Ms. Kondrat and the doorway where Gil and Margie were. Then the cracks turned into full-blown fissures. And then it was a chasm. With the next ripple, the rip in the pavement was eight feet wide and lava started pouring out. Heat engulfed me like that moment when you open an oven and your glasses instantly fog over, except way hotter. At least 1,292 degrees Fahrenheit, which is the minimum temperature of molten lava according to page 443 of *Volcanoes: A Planetary Perspective*.

I was still thinking about page 443 when Ms. Kondrat grabbed me by the collar and pulled me away moments before the lava erupted. It spattered everything with glowing confetti flames. So that wasn't good at all.

At that point, I realized three things:

1. Lava moves a lot faster in real life than it does in the movies. In films, there's always time for the hero to make a plan. In reality, there's no time to do much besides run, which is what everyone on the Promenade did.

2. Even though Third Street looks flat, it's not. It runs slightly downhill from Wilshire Boulevard to Colorado Avenue . . . which was why the lava was following us.

3. Margie and Gil had disappeared somewhere on the other side of the giant crack in the ground. I figured they were probably dead, but I didn't know if that was a fact.

My response to these realizations was to start listing every president and vice president in US history in chronological order. (You should know I do that sometimes. When I'm super stressed, my mind just kinda dumps lists and texts.)

I was up to President Zachary Taylor and his VP, Millard Fillmore, when Ms. Kondrat shook me hard by the shoulders.

"We need to run, Logan! Now!"

For once, I didn't have the urge to question Ms. Kondrat. So I began to run, which I am not good at. I have short legs and, as I've already mentioned, very limited athletic abilities. That is a fact, and it was one Ms. Kondrat seemed to notice.

"Run faster, Logan! Faster!"

I did my best while explaining to Ms. Kondrat that I've read *The Biomechanics of Elite Sprinters* by Phil Cheetham and that I know *how to run* faster. I'm simply incapable of doing it. But it quickly became clear that it's impossible to carry on a conversation when your lungs are burning from the wall of lava that's chasing you down the street.

At the intersection forty yards ahead of us, a gas-tanker truck crashed and a half-dozen other cars had smashed into each other trying to avoid it. People were desperately climbing out of and over the wreckage. Ms. Kondrat and I skittered to a stop and stared.

"We have to . . . we have to . . . we have to—"

That was all Ms. Kondrat could manage to say, and not just because she was out of breath. I couldn't blame her because the only ideas I had were bad ones, so I decided to go with the best bad idea that my brain could come up with.

"This way!" I dodged to the right, dragging Ms. Kondrat to the entrance of AgroMart, the new extreme sports store on the corner.

I'd read about the opening in the same article that featured Cornwallz Comics. According to the writer: "People waited for hours to get a free climbing session on the store's four-story rock wall during the grand opening."

But AgroMart no longer looked like it did in the newspaper. The front windows had been shattered by the earthquake. Fully outfitted mannequins lay overturned everywhere—but the rock wall was still there, with bright nylon ropes threaded to the top with a state-of-the-art auto-belay system.

And there were no lines.

"Where are we going, Logan?"

That was Ms. Kondrat again, but there was definitely not enough time to explain my plan and actually survive.

"There is definitely not enough time to explain my plan and actually survive!" I yelled to her as I grabbed the nearest climbing harness and slid it on over my legs like a self-inflicted wedgie.

"We need to harness up and climb, Ms. Kondrat. I'll tell you the rest at the top."

Ms. Kondrat stepped into her own harness, muttering to herself the whole time. "This is stupid. This is crazy." But when the first bits of lava flowed into the store's shattered front windows, she picked up her pace and put on a helmet. We started up the wall as the lava began eating away at the front of the store. Nylon clothing melted on the racks. Shelves of trail mix and nuts went instantly from raw to roasted. The sound of mini propane tanks exploding rang out every few seconds as dense, acrid smoke filled the air.

I am well aware you're supposed to drop under the smoke in a fire, but that wasn't an option in this situation. The only option was to keep climbing.

And then there were the aftershocks. Some were massive jolts that rivaled the one that split the Promenade down the middle. Others were sickening shifts that swung us on our ropes like a pair of yo-yos. The tremors rolled through at least a few times per minute, shaking the two of us off the wall again and again. But each time, the belay lines held.

We were only a few feet from the top when both of our ropes suddenly went slack. Even though there was no way to see it through the thick cloud of smoke rushing up from below, that meant the lava must have reached the bottom of the wall.

"Don't let go. If we fall at this point, nothing is going to catch us but lava!"

That was me. Ms. Kondrat started talking very loudly about me not needing to speak every thought I have right when I have it. It was a conversation we'd had before, but never on a burning rock wall, so that was new.

Moments later, I threw my leg over the top and then

helped pull Ms. Kondrat up over the edge, which was hard, because she was crying a lot and not helping as much as you might expect.

"So now what? We're going to die up here!"

"We can't die up here, Ms. Kondrat! The wall will burn and collapse first, and we'll fall to our deaths and die down there!"

Ms. Kondrat was not impressed by my logic.

"I don't want to know where we're going to die, Logan! I want to know how we're getting out of here!"

I pointed to the far side of the catwalk and showed Ms. Kondrat a door that led to a roof deck. She didn't look any happier, so I explained as we headed for the door by quoting the article.

"'AgroMart's rock wall is not much different from the ones you'd find at any climbing gym. But the way down from the top is truly unique.'"

As I finished the quote, we pushed through the door and emerged out onto a narrow deck that ran about a dozen feet to a long, braided metal wire that stretched out as far as I could see.

"A zip line?" Ms. Kondrat said it like a question, even though that's unquestionably what it was. So I just kept quoting the article while I led her over and clipped both of our harnesses into the rig.

"'AgroMart boasts the only urban zip line in Los

Angeles County. Stretching out over six hundred yards from a fourth-story roof deck, the zip line transports adventurous shoppers to the roof of a parking garage nearly three blocks east of the Promenade.'"

"Why are you talking like that, Logan? You're really freaking me out. I don't want to die with you freaking me out!"

I looked over the edge and saw that the lava was now only a few yards from the deserted gas tanker truck in the intersection. There was no more time to talk. So I double-checked we were both clipped in, then put my arms around Ms. Kondrat . . . and tackled her off the side of the building.

3:52 P.M.
FRIDAY, SEPTEMBER 17

You should know I'd never put my arms around any-one before I hugged Ms. Kondrat . . . except maybe our mother. But I wasn't thinking about our mother at all on the zip line. That is a fact.

I was thinking that the skyline of Santa Monica was whipping by outrageously fast and that Ms. Kondrat was thrashing around a lot for being forty feet up in the air.

Down below us, the wall of lava had pushed into an intersection full of crashed cars. Several of them had already started to melt. The air smelled so much like burning tires that my eyes were watering. I blinked away the tears to see that the lava was only a few feet from the tanker truck. I fully anticipated the entire intersection would explode into a supersized grill and cook us like hot dogs. But through the smoke and flames, just seconds before I expected the gas truck to blow, I saw a flash of silvery movement. And then, it looked like the lava paused for a beat before curling slightly away from the tanker. I knew it made no sense. I tried to whip my head back around and get a better look as we zipped through the smoke, but Ms. Kondrat's cardigan kept flapping in my face.

Ms. Kondrat and I sped over the top of a building and crossed Fourth Street. People were running and screaming below, and the few cars that had avoided the pileup were racing away. But we were outpacing them, and after a brief moment of reflection, I realized that that might not be a good thing.

The words of the article came back to me.

"Zip-liners can expect speeds up to twenty miles per hour as they slide, one at a time, to their destination atop the garage. 'I thought I was going to rocket right into the solid cinder block wall at the end of the line,' said Jay Davis, age eighteen, of Malibu, 'but AgroMart's adventure engineers totally know their physics. I cruised to a stop with, like, a few feet to spare.'"

I know my physics too. The zip line's speed and stopping point was calculated to work for the mass of one person; and according to the article, AgroMart had done the math right . . . for one person.

"Ms. Kondrat, I have bad news. We are not one person. That is a fact. This zip line was made for one person at a time. We are going too fast. . . . So I'm going to have to climb you. Hold your arms out and bend your knees."

Ms. Kondrat just kept staring at me . . . that is until a shock wave of airless heat slammed into us. From two blocks away, a column of fire rose into the air, higher than the nearest skyscraper. That's what happens when ten thousand gallons of gasoline ignites.

The one good thing was that explosion got Ms. Kondrat to start following directions. She straightened her arms and bent her knees so I could climb her. The wheel of our pulley was emitting a high whine like a dentist's drill. We needed a brake. That's when I remembered Anthony Rhodes's biography of Louis Renault and I bent down to grab my shoe. (In 1902, the French automaker Louis Renault created something called the drum brake that used a shoe to slow down a wheel.) With one hand holding the harness, I used my other hand to slip off my sneaker. Then I put my hand inside the shoe even though it was damp and deeply disgusting. I have sweaty feet. That's why I have never worn the same pair of socks two days in a row, even though I am an orphan.

Anyway . . . I raised my sneaker and pressed the thick part of the heel against the side of the zip line. At first, tiny ribbons of rubber came peeling off the shoe. The smell of burning latex overwhelmed the smell of smoke and gasoline. But after a few more seconds, I could tell we were slowing down.

And just in time.

The rooftop of the parking garage was less than fifty yards away. Just beyond the edge of the garage, the zip line terminated at a massive metal anchor in the side of a wall.

I leaned all my weight into my brake shoe as a few of the last wispy bits of sole flew into my face—but we slowed to a stop right over the gym mat.

That's when Ms. Kondrat started stating things loudly.

"We're alive! You did it, Logan! You saved us. You're a hero!"

She smiled. I was about to smile back when the zip line went slack and we tumbled onto the mat, Ms. Kondrat landing first with me crashing on top of her. My elbow slammed into her nose and it started bleeding . . . a lot . . . on me.

And that's when I barfed on Ms. Kondrat.

4:02 P.M.
SATURDAY, SEPTEMBER 18

Someday, whenever I find out where you are, I plan on coming to see you, no matter how far away you live. If you have a place where I can stay, that would be ideal, but I really can make almost any living situation work. I'm used to moving around a bit, even though I've lived most of my life in just one place.

I've had seven different beds in seven different rooms at the El Segundo Transitional Orphanage in the nine years I've lived there. This was not by choice. Each time I was fostered, they gave my space to a new orphan. When I'd inevitably return a week or two later, I just took whatever bed was open. I could have demanded my old bed back, but when you're an orphan who has just been unfostered, the last thing you want is to make a big deal about anything.

Anyway, my bed was never the most important thing at ESTO. The computer was. On the second floor, in the corner of the avocado-green common room where we do all of our TV watching and comic book swapping, there's a single desktop computer. It is possible the computer was kinda new back when I was just a toddler, but by the time I was about eight, it could barely get online. I've been updating it ever since then, installing new software and even replacing hard drives and motherboards when I can get the parts. You'd be surprised what computer geeks will give away to a kid who sounds like he knows what he's doing.

To be clear, I am not a computer expert. I am just good at following directions, and everything you need to know about how to update an old computer is on the internet. The trick is, you have to make sure you get that information off the internet before the computer stops working.

Timing is everything. That may or may not be a fact, but it is definitely an expression people say a lot.

However, I can say with certainty that the timing of my trip to Cornwallz with Ms. Kondrat had been particularly bad. Within a minute of us getting down from the end of the zip line, the shaking stopped entirely. No more aftershocks. No more explosions. The lava stopped flowing and began cooling in the middle of the Promenade. And once we got about a mile away, there was much less damage and all the buildings were still standing. If we had gone to the comics shop an hour earlier, we might have missed the whole thing entirely.

For the rest of the day after the quake, and all of the next morning, I spent as much time as possible on ESTO's ancient computer. Usually a good portion of my time online is spent researching . . . you. I look for any news about kids with the last name Foster or reports of kids who are one- to three-years younger than me being left by their parents in public places. I sometimes do searches for anyone who claims to have an eidetic memory in case we have that in common. The other thing I do online is find, watch, and classify cat and kitten videos. There are millions of them, but I feel nearly all of them can be placed in one of the following categories:

1. Cute cats doing adorable things.
2. Naughty cats doing hilarious things.
3. Curious cats getting themselves in trouble.
4. Talkative cats making odd noises, including some that sound like words.
5. Scared cats getting frightened.
6. Unhappy cats being unhappy, but not in ways that would hurt them permanently.

28

Some cat videos have tens of millions of views, so clearly I'm not the only one who enjoys them. I have found that my enjoyment of these videos is one of the ways I'm very much like most other people, so I sometimes use cat videos as a way of trying to connect with others. I've had mixed success with it.

Anyway . . . the day after almost dying with Ms. Kondrat, I spent less time looking for you and zero time watching cat videos so I could dedicate more time studying earthquakes in general, and the earthquake at the Promenade specifically. The thing is, nothing I found fully explained how or why it happened. I read sixty-three articles, including one that spoke about how clogged magma can cause earthquakes, which might explain why lava had poured out of the ground. Most of the articles pointed out that the Promenade Quake, as they called it, fit in with a recent trend of surprisingly strong and very focused earthquakes all over the western United States, including Nevada, Washington State, Oregon, and even as far north as Alaska. There had been a few similar ones across Southern California just in the past few days. In each case, the destruction was extreme but almost totally limited to a small area around where the epicenter was. Experts were very concerned. In several of the articles I read, Dr. Morris Williams of Caltech suggested "the trend might point toward some sort of pending cataclysmic tectonic event." Those were his exact words. It made a lot of people nervous, but not the other guys at the orphanage. They don't tend to read or watch the news very often. They have other priorities.

"Get off the computer, buttwad. I want to play BladeSniper 7."

That was Malcolm Dumont. Of the fourteen boys at ESTO, he was the only other orphan around my age. But that's where the similarities end. Ms. Kondrat has told me not to say unkind things about people, so I won't. But I will point out that he has had the same bed since he got here five years ago, and he hasn't once had to reclaim it after a placement. You can draw your own conclusions.

"What exactly is a buttwad, Mal? Do you even know what a buttwad is made of?"

Mal's eyebrows dropped, making him look even more like a modern Neanderthal.

"I dunno. It's probably a big piece of turd and stuff."

"Then why didn't you just call me a piece of turd? Or is the other 'stuff' that important?"

"Whaddya mean?"

"I was asking if you called me buttwad because you think of me as more than just a piece of turd. Should I be more offended or, in fact, slightly flattered?"

That's when Mal stopped listening, grabbed me by the back of my collar, and lifted me out of the chair so he could kill a bunch of virtual mutant soldiers with a gun that shoots buzz saw blades. That's kinda the way it works with me and Mal.

I know Mal isn't going to really hurt me and risk being sent to juvie, which is short for a juvenile detention center. Basically, kid jail. But at the same time, he knows there's nothing I can do to keep him from pushing me around if Ms. Kondrat isn't watching. So usually I just try to confuse him until he forgets to pick on me. If that doesn't work, he'll end up giving me a wedgie or making me smell his armpit. His armpits smell like dog breath, if that dog had just eaten a bag of Funyuns.

So when Mal lifted me out of the chair without subjecting me to a wedgie or lodging my nose in his armpit, I considered it a win.

I crossed the room and sat down in the only empty seat in front of the TV next to two other orphans, Jordan and Jesus. I wouldn't call them my friends, but I've known them for a while.

Jordan and Jesus were watching an Avengers movie on channel eight when the news interrupted. The reporter looked very serious and he was talking about the earthquake. There was nothing that special about either of those facts. But what he was reporting was not something I'd heard anywhere else.

"I'm Terrell McKay. Tonight, at ten, continuing

coverage of the Promenade Quake that claimed thirteen lives. We'll talk to experts who claim that bigger quakes are coming and give you tips for how to aftershock proof your home. Then we'll show you the quake video the government doesn't want you to see. Was someone . . . or something . . . in the middle of the destruction?"

"Look at that!" announced Jordan, pointing at the screen as it showed news footage of the explosion from the tanker truck. "That's the kind of thing you see in the comic books. Like when the Hulk gets all *Arggggghhhhhh-hhh!* and goes beast mode on a gas station."

Jordan and Jesus are massive comic book fans and about 70 percent of their conversations eventually turn into a debate about which hero or villain is the strongest or the coolest.

"I dunno," countered Jesus. "The lava doesn't feel like a Hulk vibe. Not green enough, anyway."

Jordan thought for a beat. "So maybe the earthquake would be the Hulk, but all the heat would be the Human Torch. Like an Avengers plus Fantastic Four collab."

"You're working too hard." Jesus shrugged. "All that mess fits more with a villain, you know, like Agent Orange."

Everyone else in the room looked confused at that point, except me, which happens a lot. So I spoke up.

"He's talking about Larfleeze," I said, "aka Agent Orange who appeared in *DC Universe* number zero in a cameo but didn't really get his own storyline until *Green Lantern* thirty-nine. He wields the power of the orange light of avarice."

Some of the other orphans nodded. Others just looked at me like I might levitate or something.

"See, brain boy knows what I'm talking about. All that bright orange lava . . . that's how Larfleeze rolls."

That was Jesus. He held his fist out, but I didn't bump it. And then they went back to arguing about which other heroes and villains were their favorites, with the older boys throwing out classic bad guy names like the Joker and Doctor Octopus, while some of the young guys tried to jump in with the newest heroes like FemmeFlorance, the Quicksilver Siren, and TideStrider.

I was more focused on the possibility of the news footage: potential proof of someone or something in the middle of the lava flow. I flashed back to what I saw while Ms. Kondrat and I were zip lining to safety. The lava seemed to stall. There was the streak of silver through the heat. I made a mental note to tune in at ten.

I'll admit, the updated death toll was the one other thing I was interested in. That probably sounds bad, but I don't mean it that way. Thirteen people had died. But they hadn't released the names of the victims. So I had been waiting for an update . . . because I was looking for the names Gil Grant and Margie Morrow.

It had been just over one full day since they had seemed

ready to ask me to come live with them. Even though I hadn't even really decided what I would've said if Earth's crust hadn't split open, it was strange that I hadn't heard from them and Ms. Kondrat hadn't either.

It probably meant one of four things:

1. They are dead . . . but the news hasn't reported it.
2. They are hurt.
3. They are missing, which means they are still either dead or hurt.
4. They just don't want to see me again.

You should know I spend a lot of time thinking about possibilities. I've been told it is not a productive habit.

But when I was thinking about why I hadn't seen Gil or Margie since the earthquake, I just kept going back and forth over those same four possibilities. *Dead, hurt, missing . . . or no longer interested.* I was still trying to decide which option was the worst when Ms. Kondrat walked into the common room and said, "Logan, there are some people here to see you."

4:11 P.M.
SATURDAY, SEPTEMBER 18

Apparently, saying "I see you're not dead" is not considered a polite way to start a conversation.

I know this because that's what I said to Gil and Margie when they turned up at ESTO, totally not dead. They weren't even injured, as best as I could tell, unless they were hiding their injuries under their shirts or pants. Margie and Gil looked just as I'd last seen them. They even had the same expression on their faces. The one that told me they were about to ask a question. But just in case I missed it . . .

"Logan, Gil and Margie have a question to ask you."

That was Ms. Kondrat, who was nodding and smiling

at me like she was trying to crush something small and hard between her lips.

"Actually," I interrupted, which I know I shouldn't, but I often do anyway, "I have a question I have to ask before they ask their question."

The adults in the room did that thing where they look at each other and raise their eyebrows to show each other they are surprised and to see if everyone else is as surprised as they are.

"It's been twenty-four hours and forty-eight minutes since I saw either of you. Why didn't you come sooner?"

I felt it was a fair question, even though Ms. Kondrat glared at me for asking it.

"Well . . . it's . . . you know, it's been a pretty *shaky* twenty-four hours . . . and forty-eight minutes . . . literally. I mean . . . literally."

That was Gil, stammering and punning.

"What Gil means," explained Margie in a more even tone, "is that after all that lava, it was chaos. We were just happy to have survived. We looked for you and Ms. Kondrat, but the fire department was clearing the area, people were still running around and panicking, and there were so many aftershocks."

"My car was . . . we couldn't . . . it was buried under a collapsed garage," offered Gil, almost apologetically. "We had to pick up a rental until insurance figures things out.

It's a minivan. It's *van*tastic."

Margie was quick to agree. "It took us forever to get home yesterday. Hours and hours. And at that point, we didn't even know if you were alive."

"And then last night . . . I got a text . . . from my boss. He called everyone in to restore the lines. I work for a telecom company. Cable, telephone, internet. Some people have a higher calling. I've got a *wire* calling."

For the third time in a row, I didn't laugh. I wasn't alone.

Margie added, "Our power was out. Both of our cell phones' batteries had died. Gil was out working; I was cleaning up the place by hand. But when the power came back on and the phone was working, the first thing we did was call Ms. Kondrat."

I looked to Ms. Kondrat. Her face was flushed.

"I may not have answered the first few times you called. The doctor prescribed rest and a mild sedative after our ordeal. There was a zip line involved, after all," she explained to Margie and Gil as if that would make it clear. It made sense to me, but I was there.

Margie knelt down and took my hands in hers.

I never really know what to do when someone touches me, unless it's an obvious situation, like they're punching me. But I didn't pull my hands away from Margie, even though I almost did.

"We wanted to come see you right away. I'm sorry it took us so long . . . and I'm sorry if you were worrying about us."

It was a good apology. I realized when she said it that I might have been worrying about them a little. I also may have been worrying about needing new sneakers since I ruined my only pair on the zip line.

"But we are here now . . . and we want to know if you'd like to come live with us . . . to be our foster child."

I've told you that I'm not always good at telling when people are joking or how they're feeling. But I'm pretty adept at telling when people are lying. I've read several books on the subject. *How to Spot Lies Like the FBI* by Mark Bouton and *Lie Catcher* by David Craig were the most recent, unless you count *Is He Lying to You?* by Dan Crum, which I found on Ms. Kondrat's Kindle a few months back.

I noticed Margie's fingers were fiddling with the zipper on her purse when she explained a few of the details of the past day. And when I asked Gil some of my questions, he looked up and to the right while he was hesitating and stammering. These are both what the books call *tells*, which are indicators that a person is saying something they know to be false. So I was confident that Gil and Margie were not being totally truthful about what had happened in the past twenty-four-hour period. Then again, most people aren't totally truthful all the time.

That is an observation, not a fact. I haven't verified that most people lie a little yet. That would take years.

But when I listened to Margie and Gil, I couldn't tell if it was just a few details that they weren't sharing or if there were giant chunks they were hiding. For all I know, they'd spent the day going door-to-door selling people fake earthquake monitors. I'd read there had been a fair amount of that kind of scam lately.

But I felt that was less likely than most of the other possibilities. Even if I doubted some of what they had said to me, I knew the last few things Margie said were true. They really were glad I was alive. They were actually sorry that it had taken so long for them to come see me. And I suppose, most importantly, they truly did want me to be their foster child.

Maybe they just needed cheap labor to help them move the bogus earthquake monitors. I didn't know at the time. All I knew was that it felt pretty good to be wanted—and it wasn't like I had a ton of other options. So I said yes.

5:13 P.M.
SATURDAY, SEPTEMBER 18

"Welcome to your new home."

That was Gil as he turned their rented Honda minivan into a driveway only two houses down from the cul-de-sac at the end of Kittyhawk Circle in Westchester, only a few miles away from ESTO. It sounded like he'd practiced saying it because it came out a bit too smooth.

He couldn't have known that every single one of the other six couples who had brought me home had said the exact same five words. I had to keep reminding myself that even though I had been through this process quite a few times, it was all new to them. I'm working on remembering that not everyone knows what I know, except I sometimes forget to work on it.

I smiled back at Gil, but I'm not very good at smiling, so I stopped after a second or two and looked down at the new shoes on my feet. I'll give Gil and Margie credit. They took one look at my beat-up sneakers and drove right to the Foot Locker and let me pick out a brand-new pair. I originally selected ones with really thick soles, just in case I ever needed another zip line brake, but Margie pointed me toward a pair of Pumas.

"These are the kind the cool kids wear at the schools where I sub. I'm a teacher."

I explained to her that I wasn't a cool kid, but I liked the sneakers and got them anyway.

When I stepped out of the minivan, two things caught my attention right away. The first was the bicycle: a metallic red hybrid that looked like it could handle urban roads or mountain trails. You should know I can handle neither on two wheels. I can't really ride a bike. Balancing is hard enough on my feet, but when wheels are involved, the difficulty jumps up several levels. I've had foster parents try to teach me, but I never lasted anywhere long enough and we never had any bikes at ESTO, so I never got any good at it.

"Do you like the bike, Logan?"

At least, that's what I think Margie said. I was too distracted by how loud it was outside to really listen. The air was filled with a low rumbling that became a heavy thundering and finally morphed into an eye watering wall of angry, hot wind. Just as Margie had started to talk, a

Qantas Airbus A380-800 jumbo jet flew right over our heads.

Kittyhawk Circle was named after the place where the Wright brothers made their famous first flight on December 17, 1903 . . . although to be fair, the flight was actually in Kill Devil Hills, which is almost four miles away from Kitty Hawk, North Carolina. That is a fact.

Anyway, the reason the street is named after the location of the first flight is because it is as close as you can get to the runway at LAX without having to go through security.

Once the noise had passed, Gil explained, "We only moved into this place a few weeks ago . . . and we're already pretty much used to the planes. Time *flies* . . . know what I mean? It's much better . . . Well, it's mostly better inside. Let's go."

With a bag containing the four sets of clothes I owned slung over my shoulder and a large stack of comic books in hand, I walked into the single-story ranch-style house. Another jet approached overhead. It looked like it was going to clip the tops of the telephone poles at the end of the cul-de-sac, but it didn't. And Gil was right. As soon as we were inside, it was much quieter, though every now and then the entire house kind of vibrated like a smartphone with the ringer turned off.

"The glass is triple paned. It really does dampen much of the sonic energy from the jets while also providing excellent insulation from the wind they generate. So that's the physics of this house *ex-planed*."

I stared at Gil. I was perplexed by several things:

1. The puns were brutal and getting worse.
2. He hadn't stammered at all during his entire technical description of the glass and insulation.
3. What he had said, aside from the pun, reminded me of something I would say.

Margie gestured to the living room and the attached kitchen.

"So this is it. What do you think?"

You should probably know things don't go well when people ask me that question because I answer truthfully, which can lead to hurt feelings. I know I've said I'm not adept at reading other people's emotions, but you should know that doesn't mean I don't care about how they're feeling. It's just that by the time I've sorted things out, it's often too late.

"I think the furniture looks brand-new and well coordinated but kind of inexpensive and cheaply stitched. The area rug should be two feet wider or a foot narrower, because right now the couch's front legs are on it, but the back ones are on the hardwood floors, which aren't really hardwood. You can tell that the patterns of knots in the boards repeat every eight feet. Oh, and the best thing in the room is the flat-screen TV. Is that the fifty- or fifty-five-inch model?"

Now it was Gil and Margie's turn to stare. I had done something Ms. Kondrat calls an over-share.

Margie's face was still kind of frozen, but Gil's broke into a smile, then a laugh. I worried that he was laughing at me, but I decided not to be offended, though I reserved the right, mentally, to change my mind.

"Gil . . . really?" I was still getting to know her, but Margie's tone made it sound like she was not happy.

"He's not wrong about any of it . . . and the TV is fifty-five inches. 4k. It's new too."

Gil and Margie showed me around the rest of the house. Almost everything had that recently delivered look, which isn't that uncommon for first-time foster parents in my experience. I think it's probably because first timers haven't had a child to scratch/stain/rip their stuff yet. Gil and Margie were my third foster family who were true first timers. First timers' houses seemed to always look undamaged . . . at least until I got there.

The kitchen in Gil and Margie's house was small, but the appliances were shiny, stainless steel, and the counters were really clean. There were two and a half bathrooms in the house, one attached to Gil and Margie's room, another one between the two other bedrooms; and off the living room was a half bathroom that Margie called the powder room.

Like I mentioned, there were two smaller bedrooms.

One was right by the door to the garage, and the other one was closer to the living room. That second one was going to be mine.

"Sometimes Gil gets emergency work calls late at night, so he has to get his gear loaded up into the van in the garage. We figured it would be quieter farther down the hall."

As if her explanation required proof, Gil took me down to the door to the garage. It was strange, because unlike most doors I've seen in the world, and totally unlike every interior door I've ever seen in a house, this one had a keypad. I've been in foster homes where certain rooms were locked, but this was quite a step up.

"Can you . . . um . . . you just have to look somewhere else, Logan."

I did as Gil asked and turned away. I heard him press a series of buttons on the keypad, eleven in all, and then the door unlocked.

"Cable piracy is a big issue, Logan. People steal channels and . . . the internet. I mean, they don't actually steal the internet, but they get free internet or commit identity theft. So my company lets me . . . I'm allowed to keep my stuff here, at home . . . and the work van so I have it. But I have to keep it locked up special. So you can't come in here without me . . . because you don't have the code . . . obviously. But you understand, right? It's . . . off-limits."

Gil kind of waved his arms across each other, as if that

might be some kind of sign language for *off-limits*. Once I nodded, he took me inside the garage and frankly . . . I wasn't at all impressed after such a big buildup.

The cable company van was there, loaded down with ladders and spools of cable. Most of the racks on the walls were covered with big toolboxes and equipment containers too. It did not look like a place where internet identity thieves would come to loot and plunder. In fact, it looked like the kind of place that could have been perfectly secure with just a sign: "Warning: Really Boring Stuff Inside."

When Gil was done showing me the garage, Margie took me to my room and left me to "get acclimated." I explained to her that there was nothing about the room that required acclimation, since the temperature was comfortable and all the furniture was already put together. She left me alone anyway and I put my clothes away. Of course, they only filled one of the drawers in the bureau. I stacked up my comics on the nightstand by my bed and put my "World's Best Big Brother" shirt under my pillow.

It took less than two minutes, and that was it. I was in my new room in my new house with my new foster family . . . and there was nothing to do. No Mal to confuse. No Ms. Kondrat to annoy with questions. No ancient computer to update. This was my new life.

Thirty seconds later, I was back in the living room. Gil was there on his laptop. Margie was clanking around in the kitchen, mumbling to herself about lima beans.

"Can I ask you something important?"

Gil looked up from his computer and Margie stopped clanking. Gil started to stammer, but Margie walked over and put a hand on his shoulder, which stopped him.

"I think I know what you want to ask, Logan, and I definitely understand. It must be strange. We're not really your parents . . . I mean, not yet. So you can just call us Margie and Gil. But if you don't feel comfortable calling us by our first names, and you want to call us Mom and Dad . . . you can. In fact, we hope you will, if not today . . . someday." She ended the sentence with a broad smile, and then she tapped Gil on the shoulder and he smiled broadly too.

I want you to know that was not at all what I was going to ask. I'm always astounded when people say things like "I think I know what you're thinking" or "I know what you're going to say." I never have any idea of what anyone else is about to say unless they're reciting lines from a book or a movie.

Anyway, I was in no mood to get into a conversation about name calling and future families.

"Margie and Gil, can I use a computer?"

Then they looked at each other in a way that was new to them, but I'd seen many times before. Six times before, in fact. It was the look of people who thought they were prepared to have me live with them, realizing that they really weren't. Finally, Gil spoke.

"We . . . we got you a bike."

5:26 P.M.
SATURDAY, SEPTEMBER 18

My brain may be capable of more storage than most people, but I was reminded just how undersized my preteen head is when I was sitting outside my new foster home trying to strap on the adult-sized bicycle helmet Gil and Margie had bought me. My question about internet access had essentially short-circuited my new foster parents. Gil promised he'd create a user ID for me a little later so I could use his laptop without having any access to his ultra-secret cable company stuff. Margie also promised to have dinner ready in a half hour. Their suggestion for me, until both of those tasks were completed, was to go ride the new bike. But before I could even attempt to ride the bike that

I'd never asked for and couldn't ride very well, I had to promise to put on a helmet with green flames on the side and far more buckles than seemed necessary.

Anyway, while I was wrangling it on and tightening straps, I noticed a very tall girl with jet-black hair and dark brown eyes walking by. She was wearing jean shorts, a tank top, and some of those strappy sandal shoes girls wear. She was really pretty, and I found myself quietly reciting the molar weights of every element on the periodic table. But what really made me take note was that she walked out of the house to the right of my new home, strolled past our house, and then went up the walkway and used a key to get into the house on the *left* of Gil and Margie's place. Then, like twenty seconds later, she came back out, now wearing a girls' volleyball uniform, and reversed the process, going from the house on my left to the house on my right, which she also entered using a key.

I started running possibilities for what I'd just seen:

1. She is a local building inspector and a part-time quick-change artist who also plays on a volleyball team after work.
2. She is a burglar who has illegal keys made for houses and then goes in to steal one outfit at a time from them.

I was well aware that neither of those explanations made any sense when she once again emerged from the first house, this time wearing a full warm-up outfit.

By this point, I must've been staring, because she stopped in front of me.

"You're staring."

Somehow, I managed to talk almost like a normal human being.

"You left that house wearing something, then you left that other house wearing something else, and then you went back and put on something different at the first house, all in less than a minute. All the clothes fit and you have keys, so I'm assuming the clothes are yours and so are the houses. I keep my clothes only in one place, so I'm confused. But then again, I only have four days' worth of clothes. Maybe you have a lot more. Most people do, I think. . . . I'm Logan. This is my house . . . sorta."

This is the point in my rare interactions with girls when they usually either laugh, walk away, or laugh as they walk away. But she didn't do any of those. Instead, she smiled and walked up to where I was standing with my gargantuan helmet. She stood there quietly for a moment while we waited for a departing MD-11 to pass.

"I'm Elena Arguello. I live next door to you."

"Which side?"

"Both."

I just stared at her, blinking occasionally.

"For most of my life, I've lived in that house." She

pointed to the house on the right. "But two and a half years ago, my parents got divorced and my dad bought that house." This time she pointed to the left.

"My folks didn't want me to have to choose which one I wanted to live with. It can get ugly, you know? So I go back and forth and it almost feels . . . I dunno . . . normal, even though it's not. But it's my life."

I nodded. I was also tempted to tell her I wasn't the right person if she wanted a ruling on what is or isn't normal. I can usually figure out what is statistically average or mathematically probable. But "normal"—that escapes me.

"So what's your deal? I didn't think Gil and Margie had a kid, but they only just moved in a few weeks ago so maybe I missed you arriving. You're not very big. With all that new furniture they bought, you could've been hiding in the credenza."

I assured Elena that I had not been stowed in any furniture and explained about being their foster kid and how we'd almost gotten burned up by lava. I also threw in my eidetic memory. I was showing off at that point, even though I wasn't exactly sure why.

"You must be really good in school, dude. What grade are you in?"

"Ninth. I'm only twelve, so I should be in seventh. But I skipped a grade in elementary school and another in middle school, mostly because none of the fourth- or

51

eighth-grade teachers in El Segundo wanted me in their classes."

Elena thought that was funny, even though I explained it was not a joke. A fact she also thought was funny. But when she was laughing at me, it didn't bother me the way it usually does.

"I'm a sophomore at Westchester High. Is that where you're gonna go?"

I hoped so. Elena seemed really nice and she was actually talking to me. The idea of seeing her every day at school and in the neighborhood after school was not unappealing. But I didn't say any of that to Elena. Instead, I just shrugged at her question. After all, school was one of many things that I hadn't really covered with Gil or Margie.

"Bet you will. Margie is a math sub there. I recognized her when she moved in. Most of the kids think she's okay. Kinda strict. Nobody messes with her."

That's when it hit me: I was going to be the underage, encyclopedic-minded foster son of a strict substitute math teacher starting at a new school almost a month into the semester. Whatever brief glow of optimism I had about sharing a school with Elena faded into the dim, unappetizing reality of how it would really be.

Elena started telling me more stuff about herself between the landings overhead—like how she had just turned fifteen, but people always thought she was older. She told me about being half Chicana because of her father, Arturo, and half Black because of her mom, Vivica. She told me about her dad's business, fixing high-end German cars in Marina del Rey, which is where many richer people live. She told me how she plays volleyball and basketball and does track and field too, and that she was All-State in all of them, but she didn't say it in a bragging way. She said it like it was just a fact.

As I listened, I was a little surprised that for once, I wasn't fixated on the details of what was being said. I was just enjoying that she was talking to me. I took the opportunity to ask her about her favorite cat videos and show her a few of my preferred ones on her smartphone. She agreed that the viral footage of an orange tabby saying "Well, hi!" with a southern drawl is top notch. I knew that once we were in the same school, and the usual stuff started happening, these moments wouldn't be very common anymore. I figured I had about thirty-eight hours before things changed. I was off by thirty-seven hours and fifty-nine minutes.

"Look who's got a new pocket-size boyfriend!"

"Yeah, it's Arguello the Giant!"

I looked down the sidewalk for the source of the jeering voices and saw a group of seven teenage boys, all wearing matching colors, walking up. Most of them looked a few years older than me as best as I could tell, and all of them had at least one item of clothing—a hat, a hoodie, or even custom sneakers—that had the letters *HSB* on them in flaming bright red.

Elena turned toward the boys and crossed her arms. All the softness went out of her face and voice.

"Very funny, Jeff. Now turn around and head back to Saul's basement before someone gets themselves in real trouble . . . not the kind that gets fixed with pressing the reset button, if you know what I mean."

I was pretty sure Elena was threatening this Jeff character. His friends seemed just as sure.

"Don't let her come at you like that, J-Hott!" The one who I assumed was Saul spoke up as the others fanned out behind him. "There's seven of us and only two of them. What are they gonna do?"

Saul's math was fundamentally correct, and in the interest of being helpful, I whispered to Elena, "You should know I will not be of much help if this turns into a street fight."

"Logan, these *boys*"—and she gestured to the clutch of teens who were now puffing up their chests—"are posers. They aren't even tough. They're a wannabe esports team . . . with no sponsor."

At that point, Jeff and Saul, who apparently were the leaders, got really loud.

"That's where you're wrong, Arguello!" Saul protested, showing off his new hat. "My man, J-Hott, got his dad's company to front us for all this new swag!"

Sure enough, when Saul held out his hat, the back of it had the logo for Hottleberger Accounting, LLC.

Jeff grinned aggressively, putting his arm around Saul's shoulder and pointing at his teammate. "That's right. And next week, my boy Salsa here has got us into a semi-professional tournament in Cerritos. Once we win that, everyone's gonna know all about the Hott Salsa Boys!"

On cue, a few of the guys started chest bumping and hooting things like "HSB for life!" and "Let's go, HSB!" They just kept on doing that . . . until they noticed how hard I was laughing.

"What's up with you, chuckles?"

That was Saul. He was not seeing the humor, so I pointed out the obvious.

"None of you guys speak Korean?"

They all stopped talking at that point—even Elena was just staring at me.

Jeff finally spoke, removing his arm from Saul's shoulder and stepping toward me as he spun his own hat around backward on his head. "What are you talking about, geek?"

"In Korean, the word *seol-sa*, which is phonetically nearly identical to *salsa*, means 'diarrhea.' So some people might think your team is the Hott Diarrhea Boys."

Now it was Saul who got super serious, maybe because he was the one who went by the nickname Salsa. His eyebrows scrunched up and he started rubbing his knuckles. "What did you just say?"

"That's not our name, nerd!" Jeff insisted, taking another step forward.

"Not to you. But to seventy-five million people in Korea, where esports is the 'national pastime' according to a 2014 *New York Times* article, you all are the Hott Diarrhea Boys. That is a fact!"

And that's when Elena started laughing.

"But if you're not very good gamers, then it's probably a sensible name. It sets expectations."

There were tears in Elena's eyes, so I kept going.

"You could tell people you don't have gaming chairs . . . you have stools . . . which is another name for feces."

That's when Jeff took three steps toward me with a raised fist, and I realized I was going to pay for making Elena laugh. There was no point ducking. It was too late.

I was trying to decide if the pain was going to be worth it when a second fist flashed by my chin and connected with Jeff's face.

Elena's long, powerful arm streaked out of nowhere and bent the boy's nose sideways, knocking his new hat clean off his head. I had no idea how she did it. I'd have sworn that a few milliseconds earlier, she was at least five feet away. But the proof was unmistakable. My face felt as normal as it ever does and Jeff's looked like someone had mushed a jelly doughnut into the space between his eyes.

Jeff and Saul's crew kept him upright as blood rolled down his chin and dripped onto his hoodie, matching the bright red of their team logo. Elena stood in front of me with her arms crossed.

"Anyone else feeling tough today?"

This was not a rhetorical question. I think she really wanted to know if any of the Hott Salsa Boys wanted to fight her. Their answer was to turn and walk away in the direction they'd come from, looking back over their shoulders to shoot us angry glances and make sure Elena wasn't following.

Once they were around the corner, Elena pulled a phone out of her pocket and then hit herself on the forehead, though nowhere as hard as she had hit Jeff.

"Dang it! I'm late for my game. I gotta run. . . ."

Before I could respond, she sprinted back to the house on the right and banged on the door twice. It was loud enough to ring out over another landing plane. Her mother, who was just as tall as Elena, came out of the door and the two hopped into a late eighties, cream-colored BMW convertible. As they drove away, Elena leaned out the passenger window.

"Welcome to the neighborhood, Logan! See you around . . . unless the Hott Diarrhea Boys get me first!"

9:36 A.M.
SUNDAY, SEPTEMBER 19

I have a vocabulary capable of describing almost anything. I've read several dictionaries and more than one thesaurus. But I don't have words for the smell I awoke to my first morning with Gil and Margie. It was distinctly acrid and septic, with a tinge of oxidized sulfur and necrotic fungus, but that still doesn't give you the full nose picture.

It turned out to be Margie's attempt at breakfast.

I found her in the kitchen, with several skillets smoking and a sink full of dishes already piled up. The evidence suggested this was not her first attempt at creating this meal.

"How do you like your eggs, Logan?"

She was probably looking for a reply like "scrambled

with cheese" or "sunny-side up," but the only answer I could manage was, "Different than how you're making them."

Gil came into the kitchen, surveyed the disaster, and suggested we go out for breakfast. I supported the idea immediately.

We all got dressed and headed out to a Denny's, where I ordered a stack of pancakes and eggs over easy, Margie got a blueberry muffin and coffee, and Gil ordered something called Moons Over My Hammy. I assumed he ordered the dish because its name was a pun, but Gil must really like scrambled eggs and ham on grilled sourdough, because I went to go wash my hands when the food arrived and his plate was clean by the time I got back.

"We wanted to take you to do some clothes shopping this morning. . . ."

That was Margie as she picked at her muffin and smiled at me. She made the smiling thing look really easy.

"After that, we can do whatever you want to do. You choose."

"Let's just *adopt* one rule: if we go to a comic book store, we stick together this time, okay?"

Gil chuckled and he was the only one. But I did appreciate the sentiment.

After we went to the mall, they took me to all the places I asked to go. No complaining. We visited the Museum of Jurassic Technology in Culver City and then headed over to the California Science Center to check out the space shuttle *Endeavor*. I wanted to confirm the 1992 Lockheed press release's claim that there are more than 26,000 silica tiles on the shuttle. For the record, there are 26,012. Finally, we drove out toward Pasadena and finished up at the Huntington Library to see the *Yongle Encyclopedia*, a unique, fifteenth-century book from China.

"Can you . . . you know . . . read Chinese, Logan?"

That was Gil, and I suppose it was a fair question. I explained to him that I couldn't read Chinese yet, but I figured I'll get around to it eventually. Then I can go back and review the encyclopedia in my memory to see what it said.

It was shaping up to be one of the top three days of my life if I was ranking them. Margie and Gil seemed really interested in what I was interested in. With the exception of cat videos, which are very popular, people are rarely interested in what I'm interested in. But I'm pretty sure Margie and Gil were because their phones went off a couple times and they didn't answer even once.

After the Huntington Library, Margie suggested we take a walk in the gardens, which are 120 acres of rare plants and trees from all over the world. Having spent some time on their website, I knew what would be in bloom, so I took Margie and Gil through the best examples.

"These are the climbing Margo Koster roses and this is the *Distictis buccinatoria*, although most people call it the scarlet trumpet vine. . . ."

I was about to explain the feeding needs of the plant when a French-sounding voice interrupted me.

"Margie and Gil, you two have the youngest tour guide I have yet to see, n'est-ce pas?"

I turned and saw a woman with brilliant green eyes and long, gloved fingers standing behind us. She was wearing a gardener's uniform with "Genevieve" stitched on to a patch. Also, you should know that while I will spell things correctly when I'm quoting her, it's just to be consistent. To hear her speak, you would think my foster parents' names were *Mar-zhee* and *Jeel*. But I don't think transcribing what she said phonetically would be very easy to read, so you'll just have to imagine the accent.

"Hey . . . wow . . . I didn't know you worked . . . I mean, of course, I knew you worked—"

The woman stopped Gil's stammering by kissing both his cheeks, which I understand is both very normal in France and kinda weird in America. But if Margie minded her husband being kissed by a woman who wasn't her, she didn't say so. In fact, she didn't say much at all.

"Genevieve. Hello. We haven't seen you in . . ."

She didn't kiss Margie, but she did smile.

"Weeks and weeks, I think. With all the earthquakes

and trouble, some of our friends voiced concerns for your well-being. But I see you two are well and enjoying *my* beautiful garden."

Even though she was not speaking directly to me, I pointed out that the Botanical Gardens were not hers. They were originally owned by railroad tycoon Henry Edwards Huntington and were meticulously laid out and realized by landscape supervisor William Hertrich. Now it was the property of the city of LA since both of them were dead, so it was unlikely this was her garden.

"Everything you say, my handsome young man, is a fact. Have you always been this smart?"

There were at least three things I liked about that sentence when she said it:

1. She called me handsome.
2. She clearly recognized facts when she heard them.
3. She asked me a question I could answer in one word.

"Yes."

Genevieve laughed. She even had a French accent when she laughed.

"So who is this brilliant boy, Gil? You must introduce us, to be sure."

Gil did a funny thing. He looked at Margie like he didn't understand what Genevieve had said to him, which was odd since her accent wasn't that thick. You should know that I'm very familiar with how people look when they don't understand what was said. I see that look when I talk all the time.

Anyway, Margie looked back at him and set her jaw. Gil spoke, stuttering more than usual.

"He's . . . well, it's . . . see . . . he's Logan . . . Foster. . . ."

"He's Gil's nephew."

That was Margie, saying something that was definitely not a fact. It was a lie.

"He's in town from Wyoming for the weekend, and he's staying with us."

I kept waiting for Gil to tell the truth, but he just nodded.

"Logan, I am Genevieve, a dear friend of your aunt and uncle. *Enchanté.* If you're only in town for such a short time, you must have a special tour. . . ."

Gil and Margie talked over each other, claiming they didn't want Genevieve to go to the trouble, but she would not take no for an answer. She took me by the hand. Her gloves were extremely soft and far more hygienic than skin-to-skin contact—a fact I very much appreciated. We strolled together through the entire Botanical Gardens, discussing all the different plants. She seemed impressed every time I knew the Latin genus and species, and a few times, she managed to tell me details about them that I'd never read before. I can honestly say she knew everything about every single one of those plants. Plus, she smelled really good too.

The sun was setting by the time we got back to the entrance.

"We really do have to get going."

That was Margie, who hadn't said much in the previous few hours.

"Of course. What was I thinking? Young Logan has a flight to catch back to Montana, was it?"

I saw Gil and Margie looking at each other once again.

"Wyoming," I interjected, not lying, but restating what I'd heard and elaborating. "Gil said I was here from Wyoming before, but it's close to Montana, and the two states do share three hundred and fourteen miles of border."

Genevieve bent down and kissed both sides of my face. I was too stunned to react other than to continue muttering facts about Wyoming and Montana from an almanac I'd read once.

"You are a brilliant and charming boy, Logan. Your aunt and uncle . . . they are lucky to have you, even for a short visit. I hope you will return to this garden anytime you come back . . . from Wyoming."

Then she turned to Gil and Margie.

"And you two, I hope it will not be so long before I see you again, my friends."

And with that, Genevieve gave us a wave and headed back toward the greenhouse. Gil and Margie led me back to the car, and only once we were out of earshot did they speak to me. And at that point, they were both speaking simultaneously.

"Logan, I'm so sorry . . ."

"Thank you for . . . you know . . . I mean . . ."

"I'm sure you're a bit confused."

"Genevieve is someone we both worked with . . . sort of . . ."

"She knew about our trouble having a child of our own . . ."

"She . . . and the . . . well, we have friends in common . . . and . . ."

"We never told them we were looking into adoption. We kept that to ourselves."

"We kinda panicked . . . back there . . ."

Margie held a finger out. Gil seemed to understand that meant he had to stop talking.

"Logan, our plan was to introduce you to our friends once you're more acclimated to living with us. We don't want it all to be too much at once. And here it is, your first full day as part of our family—our foster family—and we ran into someone we didn't expect to see. I knew that if we told her you were our son—"

"Foster son," I corrected her, because accuracy is important.

"Yes, foster son. If she knew, she'd tell our other friends

66

and they'd all want to meet you and we didn't want you having to deal with that so soon."

Gil just nodded along.

"You understand?"

I told them I did because I understood their explanation. I didn't tell them I believed them, though, because I didn't. By this time, I was very familiar with their tells.

I wasn't sure why they had lied, but the most likely possibilities were the following:

1. They were embarrassed or ashamed of their friend Genevieve.

2. They were embarrassed or ashamed of me.

Considering how nice and smart and French Genevieve was, I knew which one it was.

That might seem like an opinion, but really it was a fact.

6:08 P.M.
FRIDAY, SEPTEMBER 24

Have you ever thought about what job you might want when you're older? I've spent some time on it. Logically, being a librarian would make sense. I'd have access to so many books and always know exactly where each one goes without even needing the Dewey decimal system. I suppose being a fact-checker for a news organization would make sense too. I do appreciate facts. That is a fact. And, of course, I've thought about being a scientist. I'd consider any field but meteorology. It's just too unpredictable. Even the US government's own website (SciJinks.gov) admits that beyond a week, forecasts are only right half the time. Conversely, my own forecast for my first full week at school was flawless.

Within a few days, I was known as the "crazy smart, totally weird new kid" at Westchester High. Those were not my words, but I heard three different girls in my homeroom use them in reference to me. I've been that kid before, so I was prepared. I also had several teachers who hadn't ever taught a "crazy smart, totally weird new kid" before, which meant they were not prepared for when I'd correct them in class or quote the textbook verbatim. A few seemed impressed. I could tell because they were the ones who didn't kick me out of class, accuse me of cheating, or send me to see the guidance counselor.

Speaking of the guidance counselor, I'm pretty sure he's an ex-military type. After the third time I got sent to him, he mentioned that the CIA are recruiting kids like me. I told him I'd be willing to consider it just for the opportunity to meet the other recruits. There are plenty of other neurodivergent people in the world, but so far I've never encountered anyone that seems quite "like me" when it comes to my memory or my circumstances.

One thing is for sure. There were no kids like me at Westchester High. The only people who seemed glad to see me were the AcaDemons, the school's National Academic Quiz Tournaments team. But people were lining up to be the opposite of friends, especially the Hott Diarrhea Boys. On day one, they defaced my name tag with a Sharpie, so it read "Hello, I'm Logan Fartster." I was required to wear it for the entire day according to paragraph 32 in the

Westchester High new student handbook. Then Jeff and Saul created a fake Instagram account for "Logan Fartster" with my face on it and used it to follow everyone at school.

I wasn't able to shut it down until the end of the day. Gil had given me a flip phone he got for free from work, so I could barely text, let alone get online. I figured Jeff wasn't very creative or security minded, so as soon as I got home, I went on Gil's laptop and just tried every sequence or letters and numbers I had seen on the Hott Salsa Boys' custom clothing, which I memorized the day we met. "HSB4LYFE" was the password.

Still, the damage was done. Even the AcaDemons were scared off. The only person who didn't treat me like I was toxic was Elena. She said hi in the hall and she even ate lunch with me before running off to volleyball practice.

I'll admit that having a cool and popular person pay attention to me was a welcome change, even if I was sure it wouldn't last.

To be fair, I wasn't the only one having a bad week. There were more of those weird, super-focused earthquakes popping up across Los Angeles. Lots of them. Every day there were tremors and reports of more buildings and roads that were heavily damaged throughout Southern California. Several homes fell into actual holes in the ground. Experts insisted the pattern of all these quakes did not resemble any fault map they were aware of.

The school wasn't damaged by any of them, but we had three separate occasions when the epicenters were close enough that we had to evacuate until there was an all clear bell. On the last of the three evacuations, Margie was subbing at the school that day. I looked for her when we were all standing on the athletic field, waiting to be let back into the building. It's not like I expected her to abandon her class and come check in on me. That would be foolish and possibly endanger her position as a substitute teacher. But I figured she'd give me a wave or something . . . except she didn't seem to be present. I couldn't see her anywhere, which I thought was also something that would definitely endanger her position as a substitute teacher.

When she and I met up after school, she insisted I must have missed her in the crowd. The thing is, with my memory, even if I do "miss" something, I can go back and "see" what I missed. She wasn't there.

If I sound like I was suspicious of my new foster parents, it's because I was. I've learned that a little suspicion is useful and keeps you from being totally surprised when foster parents ask you to commit mail fraud or when they drop you back near (but not actually at) the orphanage.

So I kept track of the details I couldn't exactly explain with Margie and Gil. For example, Gil never ate with us. That is a fact. Margie was a horrific cook, so I thought that might be why Gil always had an excuse. In the morning, he said he was going to meet up with the other cable guys for doughnuts. At night, he'd have equipment to catalog or paperwork to do while we ate. He was always promising to reheat his dinner later.

But I never heard the microwave beep after I went to bed. The sink got turned on and the trash disposal was run, but no beeping. In a modern kitchen, there is almost no way to reheat food without some sort of beeping.

Another time, I wanted to use Gil's laptop to catch up on some cat videos and also look for you. (It wasn't like I gave that up when I was fostered.) The computer wasn't out in the living room, so I had to go into their bedroom, where I found it on the nightstand. I was just going to take it and leave, but the closet door was open. All Margie's clothes were hanging neatly enough. Gil's clothes were there too, but something about the way they were hanging . . . they looked different. That's when I saw the dust. There was dust on all Gil's clothes. Not a lot, but Margie's didn't have that same coating. I didn't know what it meant. Why would his clothes be dusty and hers wouldn't? So I started coming up with possibilities:

1. Maybe his cable installation job got him coated in dust and when he hung up his clothes, that dust sometimes settled on his other clothes . . . and only his other clothes.

2. Maybe there was a raccoon in the crawl space

above the closet on his side, and when it
moved around, it knocked dust down onto
his clothes.
3. Maybe Gil had extreme body odor and used
a powdered all-over deodorant to mask it.

None of these explanations seemed all that reasonable.
But that wasn't even all of it.

The food in the house was all brand-new. Mustard,
juice pouches, pretzels, soy sauce, American cheese
singles . . . every one had to be opened for the first time
when I asked for them. The expiration dates confirmed
it. I knew that they'd just moved in and probably had to
restock after the earthquake, but it seemed bizarre that
there wasn't *something* that hadn't just been bought.

Also, there weren't any pictures of Margie from when
she was young. There were a few of Gil as a boy and as a
nerdy dude in college, but I have no idea whether Margie
grew up as a nerd or a cheerleader or a goth with nose
rings. There were no pictures of her where she didn't look
like her current self. No photo albums either. I looked for
a photos folder on Gil's laptop, but didn't find anything.
Who doesn't have a bunch of pictures on their computer, I
mean other than me? But then I've never owned my own
computer or camera.

Anyway, toward the end of that first week, I went into
the kitchen where Margie was chopping up carrots into
a pot of soup. It smelled kinda like clam chowder, but it

looked more like split pea. By that point, I was used to Margie's cuisine. I didn't enjoy it, but I was used to it and I did appreciate the effort. I'd never seen anyone work so hard at making inedible food.

"Dinner won't be ready for another half hour. But if you're starving, there's some cheese in the fridge and crackers above the toaster."

She was right: an entire block of unopened Colby Jack and a sealed box of Triscuits.

"Margie, how come there are no pictures in the house of you when you were younger?"

Margie turned her attention away from the carrots as she raised her eyebrows, but her hands kept working with the knife.

"You noticed, huh?"

I could have told her that I noticed all kinds of things, like how strange it was that a truly awful cook like her could chop vegetables without even looking at her hands. In 2018, the National Electronic Injury Surveillance System reported that kitchen knife injuries send over 322,000 people to the ER each year. Yet Margie appeared totally unfazed by the danger posed by the eleven-inch knife that kept rising and falling just millimeters from her hand.

Of course, I didn't point that out because I didn't want to change the subject.

"It just seemed weird since there are pictures of Gil."

"Well, I was raised in a very different way than most people, Logan. My parents were from someplace very far away, and they didn't take pictures where we were from."

"Are you Amish? I've read the Amish interpret the second commandment's prohibition of graven images as forbidding photography."

"No, I'm not Amish. It wasn't so much religious as cultural. We just didn't have . . . cameras. But when I got older and moved here, and I met Gil . . . well, you've seen those pictures."

I had, and I had noticed something else.

"Is that why your parents aren't in your wedding portraits?"

This time, Margie put down the knife, leaned up against the edge of the stove, and she looked sad. At least, I think she looked sad. It certainly looked less happy than her usual face.

"I lost them both a few years before I met Gil. I had a sister but . . ."

Margie never finished the sentence. We both just kind of stood there, me with a half-prepared plate of cheese and crackers, her with a cutting board full of carrots. I think I felt bad for being suspicious of Margie. That's what had led me to ask her about the pictures, which had gotten her talking about her family. I know how it feels to talk about a family you don't have, and I did not mean to make her feel that way.

I was just about to try and say something to make her feel better, which I'm not very good at, when I noticed her arm was leaning up against the hot pot of soup . . . and it wasn't hurting her. Instead, it was making her elbow look silvery where it was close to the heat.

I was so surprised, I forgot to say anything to make her feel better. I just took my crackers and cheese in the other room, put them down next to the laptop, and started googling "silvery skin." There were 7.35 million results. That is a fact. The links ranged from rare skin disorders to comic books to profiles of fish. I read as many as I could before dinner was ready . . . but there was nothing that made any sense.

I can put up with a lot of things: no parents, school bullies, earthquakes, oversized bicycle helmets . . . you name it. But living in a place where nothing makes sense? It was just too much.

5:19 P.M.
WEDNESDAY, OCTOBER 6

The next week and a half were full of more earth-quakes, more bullying by the Hott Diarrhea Boys, and a lot more poorly kept secrets from Gil and Margie. They seemed distracted and were always whispering about me. People whisper about me frequently. People diagnosed with Autism Spectrum Disorder often have strong auditory sensitivity, so maybe they think I might have superhearing. I don't, which is too bad.

Anyway, Gil was working really long hours. Some days he left before I woke up and didn't get home until after I was in bed. I caught up to him one morning because I wondered if the added financial burden of having me in the house was the reason for all the overtime.

"Is the added financial burden of having me in the house the reason for all the overtime?"

"No, Logan, it's not like that. We're okay . . . better than okay with you being here. It's the earthquakes . . . the damage to the cable lines. Someone's got to clean things up . . . like I always say, *wire* we working if not to fix cable . . . it's a work joke. You understand, right?"

I did, but I still didn't believe him. I noticed that Gil stammered whenever he talked about anything that wasn't technical, but he was even more stammerish when he wasn't telling the truth.

On my third Wednesday with Margie and Gil, I was sitting on the front step a little before sundown when Elena came out of the house on the left wearing a Lakers jersey and short jean shorts. They did not look practical for playing basketball.

"Quick, how many points did Shaq score on November twenty-first, 1999?"

It's not like Elena didn't believe I had an eidetic memory. She just liked testing it out, specifically about Lakers stats.

"Thirty-seven on fifteen for twenty-five shooting, but the Lakers lost to the Raptors by nine. That is a fact."

Elena came up the walkway to the house and gave me

a fist bump and sat down next to me. "My dad's taking me to the game tonight. Hope they don't lose like they did on November twenty-first, 1998."

"It was 1999, which was also the year artist Frances Stark began recording a series of videos of her cats, seven full years before the first cat video was uploaded to You-Tube," I corrected her and immediately wished I hadn't, but she didn't get mad. That's the cool thing about Elena. She gets that I can't always control that kind of thing.

"Can I ask you a question? I mean, another question since technically, I already asked you one?"

That was me, trying to sound like a normal person. Elena laughed and shook her head, and when she did, her hair kind of swished around. Then I forgot what I was going to ask her, which is something that almost never happens to me.

"Go ahead, Logan. Ask away. Ask three questions if you want."

I remembered what I was going to ask. "Your parents leave you home alone, right?"

"Of course. Why, don't your folks—I mean, Gil and Margie?"

"No. I mean yeah, they do. What I really meant is do your parents ever go out and leave you . . . at night. Like *overnight* or, you know . . . in the middle of the night?"

She pressed her lips together and tilted her head down

at me. I think some kids call it the duck face. Elena could never look like a duck. She's much too pretty to be compared to a waterfowl.

"Logan, are you messing with me?"

I smiled and I explained to her, "Yeah, I'm messing with you. Totally messing with you. I do that sometimes. It's like a hobby."

I wasn't messing with her. I just realized at that moment that I couldn't tell her about the night I woke up at 2:13 a.m. with a nosebleed. I get them sometimes, especially when it's dry and the Santa Ana winds are blowing. As my little brother or sister, you shouldn't worry about me and my nosebleeds, if you were. It's pretty common. The website of the Cleveland Clinic estimates about 60% of people have at least one nosebleed in their lifetime.

But when I woke up with a bloody nose that night, I got up and went to the bathroom. On the way down the hall, I noticed Gil and Margie's door was slightly open, and when I listened, there was no snoring . . . not even any breathing. So I poked my head inside and saw that there was no one sleeping in the bed. Margie's side had the covers all pushed back, but no Margie. Gil's side hadn't been slept in at all.

I walked through the whole house, except for the keypad-locked garage, and found no one else at home. The strangest thing, though, was that when I looked outside, the minivan was still parked in the driveway. I figured Margie might have left with Gil in his work van, though that didn't make much sense, since he wasn't even home when I went to bed. Then I started thinking of other possibilities:

1. She could have left on foot.
2. She could have been picked up by a friend.
3. She could have been picked up by a boyfriend.
4. She could have been abducted by aliens . . . or a cult . . . or ninjas . . . or a cult that worships alien ninjas.

Like I've said before, it's not good when I have too much time to think about the possibilities.

I went back to my room and waited, but at some point I fell asleep. When I woke up, Gil and Margie were both home, looking normal and relatively well rested, while I looked like a zombie from being up half the night.

I didn't say anything to them then, and I didn't tell any of that to Elena in the front yard either. It wasn't that I didn't trust her. I just knew that if I did tell her, she might feel she had to tell someone else. Then the Department of Social Services might get called. I didn't need the DSS in this case. I just needed some answers.

Then I heard Margie calling me from inside. At least, I thought I did. Apparently so did Elena.

"Wow, she must be really yelling if we can hear her

through that triple-paned glass."

It was a good point. But before I could comment, the front door opened.

"Logan! Can you come inside? Gil and I wanted to talk to you about— Oh, hi, Elena! Looks like you're dressed for the game tonight."

"Heading to the Staples Center in a few minutes, Ms. Morrow."

"You know you can call me Margie when we're not at school, right?"

Elena smiled and nodded. "Gotta run. I'll see you at school tomorrow, Logan."

I waved feebly. I wasn't so sure I would see her at school. I kept hearing Margie's partial sentence rerunning in my head. "Gil and I wanted to talk to you about . . ."

It sounded like they wanted to talk about something serious. I thought maybe they were ready to share whatever they had been keeping secret. That would be very helpful. On the other hand, maybe they wanted to talk about sending me back to ESTO. After all, every other time foster parents have had that conversation with me, it started much in the same way.

When I got inside, I was already mentally preparing to pack the new clothes Margie and Gil had bought for me, just in case. But that's when they surprised me.

"Gil is taking tonight off and we were thinking about going to the movies all together. There's a new action movie that's playing at the HHLA theaters."

This wasn't the conversation I was expecting to have.

"Yeah . . . it's supposed to have great special effects . . . 3D with the glasses. . . ."

That was Gil, sounding like he was actually pretty excited to see it. "It's called *ThunderPulse Returns*. . . . It's a sequel, but you know those superhero movies. They're just an escape . . . emphasis on the *cape*. . . . It's not like you need to know the backstory."

He's right, but I still spent the whole car ride recounting ThunderPulse's exact backstory to them anyway. I covered his origin on the way to the theater. While we waited in line, I explained his secret identity. While we got popcorn, I explained his powers, which include being able to turn sound into electricity and vice versa. The funny thing is, ThunderPulse's comic books aren't even my favorites, even though I'd read them all. It just felt good just to talk about something other than what I thought we were going to be talking about. So I kept going until we sat in our seats.

"Logan, before the movie starts, we actually wanted to talk to you about something else."

Margie was looking right at me, and Gil was too, except he kept shooting glances to Margie as well. She finally looked back at him and he spoke.

"We're wondering . . . do you, you know . . . um . . . like, living with us?"

"I like it compared to a lot of the foster homes I've been in. You guys don't yell ever, and I don't think you're using me to get extra aid from the state. So that's good."

Margie followed up the question with another.

"Do you like it more than when you were living at the orphanage?"

"It's different. I like having my own room. The food is . . . well it's nice to be able to get snacks whenever I want them. But at ESTO, I had a better idea of what was going on."

Gil and Margie looked at each other, seemingly perplexed. But I thought it was a pretty unambiguous statement by me. Gil offered a guess at what I was talking about.

"Do you mean you had . . . you know . . . a routine? And, um . . . friends?"

"No. I mean I knew what was going on. I knew when Ms. Kondrat was going to show up and when she'd go home. I knew what the other orphans were up to, even the ones that were up to stuff they shouldn't be. And when they were lying to me, I knew why."

Gil acted like he didn't know what I was talking about. I hate it when people do that.

"What are you . . . you seem like . . . I mean, you know what we do every day. You're in the house with us . . . or outside. You spend a lot of time outside. We thought maybe you don't like the house. So that's why we decided we should talk . . . here."

The previews started to play, and I knew we really didn't have time to drag this conversation out. So I spoke as plainly as I could.

"When do you eat, Gil? I mean, when do you *really eat*? Will you eat some of this popcorn right now?" I held up the gigantic tub they'd bought for us.

Gil opened his mouth, but nothing came out, and nothing went in either.

"Margie, where were you that day when they evacuated the school?"

Margie frowned.

"Why is every package of food in the house brand-new? Why are the clothes in Gil's closet dusty, like they've never been worn? Does Margie have some strange metal prosthetic arm?"

I asked more questions. Several previews' worth of questions until Margie put her hands up to her mouth. I could hear a catch in her voice, although I'm pretty sure she was just talking to herself.

"This isn't how this was supposed to be. We should just tell him. . . ."

Gil finally found his voice.

"Logan, I know you have lots of questions, and Margie and I . . . we want to answer them . . . but it takes . . . it takes time and effort. We have to . . . build trust. But if you'd rather . . . I mean . . . if you don't want to live with us . . ."

"Maybe we should just go and talk somewhere else—"

That was Margie. But before she could finish the sentence, the movie started. The lights got dimmer, everyone put on their 3D glasses, including me, and we had to stop talking.

That was fine with me.

Margie and Gil hadn't planned this out well. You can't have big conversations in a place where you're going to have to stop talking for several hours. It just doesn't make sense. But I figured I'd at least get to watch the movie before telling them I was ready to go back to ESTO. Maybe they still kinda wanted me to stay, or maybe they were just trying to make themselves feel better by asking what I wanted. I don't know, and I'm not even sure they did either. But it was definitely clear they weren't going to tell me the truth. I'd given them several chances and they had taken exactly zero of them. So since this was going to be my last night as their foster son, and I don't get to go to the movies much at the orphanage, I decided I'd try to enjoy it.

The big opening scene started and I looked at Gil and Margie for a second in the dark. The light bouncing off the screen making their seemingly sad faces glow. Neither of them had their 3D glasses on. Margie had silvery tears in her eyes; at least that's how it looked with the screen reflecting in them. Gil was holding her hand and looking at me like he expected me to say something.

But the movie had started. There's no talking during a movie. That is a fact. ThunderPulse was there, surrounded by evil battle droids. He started charging up his powers, getting ready to level them with a sound-fueled electricity blast. Gil was right. The visual effects were unreal. But I remember thinking that the sound system was even better. The floor was shaking with each explosion. Every time ThunderPulse cut loose, everything rumbled so much it felt like the seats were going to tear out of the ground.

But when the last battle droid was obliterated, the shaking didn't stop. In fact, it got stronger . . . and stronger.

That's when a beefy guy wearing a purple costume, with blue metal bands around his head and wrists, exploded through the screen on a jet-powered hoverboard. It was like he was actually radiating power, and I could hear the bolts on the bottom of my seat start to creak and strain. He banked hard into the theater and looked around, as tiles started falling from the ceiling and exploding on the aisle floors. But then his eyes found my row and he shouted right at me, Margie, and Gil.

"Found you!"

I turned and saw Gil and Margie looking up with their mouths open like they were surprised. But then they both stood, and their expressions changed.

"Get Logan and get out of here!"

That was Gil, barking orders to Margie, his stutter gone. "I'll deal with Seismyxer. Go!"

7:42 P.M.
WEDNESDAY, OCTOBER 6

Before I could even comment, Margie hoisted my entire body off the seat and carried me away in one arm, toting me as easily as if I were a package of toilet paper. I did my best to look around and realized that people all through the theater were screaming, running for the exits.

And then I saw something flash upward, like a light streak into the projector's beam. Suddenly, Gil was on the hoverboard, grappling with the man riding it. But Gil didn't look quite like Gil. He wasn't wearing what he'd been wearing a second before. He had on a skintight suit with an insignia on the chest. It looked like a Q but also sorta like a hydrogen atom. I didn't get a great look at it because the entire room shook again. A wave of energy came out of the guy with the metal bands. And then Gil disappeared. I mean literally—like he was blown apart as if he had been made of sand.

I shouted something that started with "holy" and ended with a second word. It was a bad word so I'm not going to write it here because you're my younger sibling. But it got the bad guy's attention. Another pulse of energy erupted out of him and it rippled toward us. Margie swung me around and shielded me with her back just before the chairs and the wave of energy slammed us, pushing us airborne and out the doors of the theater.

As we flew through the air, it felt like slow motion. Margie held me so tightly I almost couldn't breathe. I noticed that Margie's skin didn't look like skin. It looked like metal: polished, silvery metal. Her whole body too—from her face to her hands. And as we were hurtling toward the base of the concessions counter in the lobby, the last thing I remember thinking before we hit the ground was *My foster parents are superheroes. That is a fact!*

I don't know if I technically lost consciousness right after that, or if my brain simply shut down and rebooted. But the next thing I knew, Margie was cradling me in the outdoor atrium in front of the theater. Then I heard a gigantic smash that made me sit up straight. There were windows breaking and walls exploding out from the front of the theater, and through the cloud of dust and glass,

I could see Seismyxer searching the lobby and leveling anyone or anything that got in his way. People trampled out around us, stumbling as the ground churned and shifted underneath their feet.

Margie's skin was back to normal, but her clothes were pretty much destroyed. I was a little embarrassed for her. Then she started tearing off what she had left on while yelling out, "Gil!"

I'd just seen Gil vaporized, so I thought she might be having a breakdown right there on the street.

But she knew exactly what she was doing, as she revealed an actual superhero uniform underneath her clothes: a silver bodysuit with a glowing red *QS* on the front.

"You're Quicksilver Siren?" I asked Margie, but then before she could answer, Gil appeared next to her.

That is not a figure of speech, by the way. He seriously materialized out of nothing.

"Seismyxer is like a rabid dog in there. He'll bring down the entire theater on top of everyone in it if he thinks it'll take us out."

Margie took a step back toward the building like she was ready to fight. But Gil put his hand on her shoulder. "There are too many people still inside. We need to get Seismyxer away from the crowd," Gil insisted. "There's a parking garage under construction around back. . . ."

Just then, Seismyxer erupted out of the theater as the marquee detonated, sending a shower of sparks all over everyone. It made Margie's skin turn metallic. She looked like she was entirely made of mercury.

It was really cool and just like the comic books.

In the first edition of the Quicksilver Siren comics, it was explained that she was from Aznasch, a planet eight-trillion light-years away. Aznasch's gravity was five times that of Earth, and the planet's proximity to a white dwarf star caused the temperature to rise to seventeen-hundred degrees during the day. Her race had evolved with super-dense cells to survive in the conditions. Quicksilver Siren's epidermis was made of molten metal suspended between layers of silicone skin. At room temperature, the silicone shielded the metal. But when her skin comes into contact with high temperatures or blunt force . . . quicksilver.

"To the garage! Now!"

That was Margie shouting as she pointed Gil toward the back of the shopping complex. "Logan, get as far away as you can. We'll find you after. I promise!"

Gil gave me a nod, and then he became a light streak that arced toward the garage. At the same time, Margie bounded out and jumped up onto the hoverboard to wrestle Seismyxer as he chased Gil.

As they flew away, I swear I could hear Margie's voice saying, *You don't want to hurt anyone*, over and over again.

It took me a second to realize her voice wasn't meant for my ears. She was trying to get it into Seismyxer's head. That's the *Siren* part of her hero name. On Aznasch, the air gets too hot to carry sound, so her race also developed the ability to communicate telepathically. When she arrived on Earth, she found that she could still speak with her mind, but when she broadcast her telepathy out with a bit of intensity, it had persuasive effects on humans.

I know . . . super cool, right? I wanted to ask her about it, but I was suddenly alone (even though I was in the middle of hundreds of people running for their lives). Anyone with any sense was sprinting as fast as they could away from the garage. I should have joined the crowd like I was told, but I didn't. I had to know that what I saw was really real.

I ran around behind the theater and looked up at the third floor of the unfinished parking garage. It was like a rave was going on; there were brilliant flashes of light and repeated subsonic booms. Bits of dust and debris flew out of the openings.

When I finally got to the third floor, it was like a scene out of the movie we'd originally gone to see. Gil flashed around almost faster than I could follow, bouncing from walls to the ceiling to right up in Seismyxer's face. Whenever Seismyxer's blasts hit Gil, he'd vaporize briefly before re-forming. He seemed unkillable, but he definitely wasn't winning the fight either. Margie was silver from head to toe. She dodged force waves as Seismyxer blasted them her way, blowing out the walls behind her. Margie was totally focused on Seismyxer, but her telepathy was still affecting me. I kept hearing her voice in my head saying things like *Surrender!* and *Let down your guard.*

Seismyxer tapped the metal band at his temples and roared at Margie, "I can hear you . . . but thanks to my cool new headband, you ain't the boss of me! There's nothing you can say to keep me from putting you and your hubby in the ground!"

Whatever power he had to cancel out Margie's telepathy, it only worked for him. Because at the same time he was mocking her, I found myself wanting to surrender and let down my guard, which is why I shouted out.

"Okay! I surrender! My guard is down!"

Suddenly, all three of them looked at me and I wished I hadn't said anything.

"I don't leave witnesses, kid!" Seismyxer gestured in my direction and suddenly, the concrete between us started to ripple up like a wave in a surfing competition. It was going to crash over me; but a millisecond before the ground exploded toward me, something lifted me away and whipped me over to Margie. It was only when I stopped moving that I realized I was in Gil's arms.

"What just happened?"

That was me, but my foster parents didn't answer the question right away.

"Are you okay, Logan?" Gil asked as he put me down.

"Why didn't you run like I told you to?" Margie demanded. I could see her eyebrows slanting down and her lips tightening up. It was a look I'd seen from other foster moms, just never from one with an all-silver face.

Before I could answer, there was a thundering rumble. The floor of the entire parking garage was rolling toward us like another ocean swell. And then we were all airborne again, tossed up by the wave and catapulted out of the unfinished garage into the night air.

We fell, and I watched as the top two floors of the garage crumbled and began to fall as well, with huge chunks of concrete chasing us toward the ground.

That's when Margie reached out and pulled me in close, at which point I held on to her too. I realized it was technically my second hug in the space of a month—and both of them happened several stories up in the air. It seemed like a coincidence, but I figured it was a pattern worth noting before I plummeted to my death.

Anyway . . . next thing I knew, Margie and I were no longer falling. Instead, we were moving impossibly fast in tiny little bursts. Each little burst of speed felt like my skin was being pulled off my body. It was not pleasant. But after the first few bursts, I could see we were zooming away from the garage and Seismyxer, with me yelping every half second or so. A minute later, we stopped in an underpass on the northbound 405. Gil reappeared, exhausted from carrying us as he collapsed onto the concrete a few feet away.

"Are you all right?" Margie asked him as she put me down.

"Tired . . . real tired . . . Had to get us away fast . . . and far. Seismyxer figured out we'd protect Logan."

"He figured more than that. My telepathy was doing nothing. . . ."

"And he knew the exact frequency that would disrupt my atomic bonds. . . ."

"He knew where to find us and that we're married. How is that possible?"

"Hey!"

I know I have a bad habit of interrupting, but I don't yell often. On May 8, 2008, Professor Clinton Richard Dawkins, an English evolutionary biologist, wrote, "Anybody who has something sensible or worthwhile to say should be able to say it calmly and soberly, relying on the words themselves to convey his meaning, without resorting to yelling." I agree with that in general, but this was not a time for *calmly* or *soberly*.

"I've got questions too—and I need answers right now."

10:19 P.M.
WEDNESDAY, OCTOBER 6

I'm sure that when we finally are face-to-face, you and I will both have lots of questions and information to share. I already have a list of 472 questions I want to ask you, ranked by importance. I will not ask them all at once, but I do hope we'll be able to have that conversation somewhere comfortable, like a living room or maybe a diner. Almost anyplace other than a noisy, windy freeway underpass. It's just not well suited for important discussions.

But that's exactly where I found myself with my super foster parents, for 126 of the oddest minutes of my life.

"You're really the Quicksilver Siren?" I asked Margie, even though I had seen her using most of her powers. I felt it was important to get her on record.

"Yes. That's what people call me when I'm like this."
She gestured to her costume and her skin, which was
returning to normal flesh color. "But I'm also Margie, your
foster mother, and I think that's what you should call me."

"Are you really from the planet Aznasch, sent to study
our planet and then marooned when your spacecraft
crashed into the Grand Canyon?"

Margie sighed and crossed her arms until it was clear I
was serious about getting answers. "Yes, here to study the
planet. Yes, marooned. No to the spaceship. I was trans-
ported via wormhole, which closed when a binary system
went nova in the Vega galaxy. No, not from Aznasch . . . my
planet's name can't be pronounced using human tongues.
When you become a hero, they change some stuff. . . ."

I turned to Gil and asked, "And who are you?"

"I'm Gil." He responded, before realizing what I was
actually asking. "But they call me Ultra-Quantum. At
least . . . so far, Ultra-Quantum. I was going to be *Dr.
Quantum* but they figured that brings up too many questions. You know—'What kind of doctor' or 'Where did he
get his degree?'"

"There's no Ultra-Quantum comic book. There's no
Dr. Quantum either," I pointed out.

"I'm new. I haven't had my powers all that long and
they haven't decided . . . Well, not everyone gets a comic
book. Besides, it's unlikely people will ever really see me

because of what I do . . . or what I can do. I'm still figuring it out a little."

Gil kind of looked down and Margie put a hand on his shoulder.

"What are your powers? How did you get them? What happened when that Seismyxer guy blasted you into nothingness? Where did you go? Are you immortal? Is that why you don't eat?"

I went on like that for quite a while. At first, they answered my questions patiently, but eventually I heard Margie's voice in my head telling me to pipe down. Having a foster mom who can influence your thoughts telepathically seems like an unfair advantage. Anyway, I stopped talking, and Gil explained.

"I was a scientist . . . a professor of quantum mechanics . . . and I was studying the advanced technology that Margie's planet used to send her here. That's how we met and . . . you know, Margie and I . . . Well, I thought she was *out of this world*. Sorry. Anyway, they called me in to help replicate the wormhole . . . exciting molecules of dark matter with neutrino rays. I guess I should explain—"

"No need," I assured him. "I read *Dark Matter's Place in the Universe and Microverse* from the Global Astrophysics Summit in Geneva in 2000. It is one of the seven most boring things I've ever read. That is a fact, and I've read the dictionary."

"Oh, okay . . . good. Easier that way. Anyway, my containment calculations were off, and the lab was compromised. I was able to get everyone out and seal the doors, but when I activated the gravitational magnet to recapture the dark matter, the loose neutrinos passed through my body on the way to the magnet. This should have either done nothing to me . . . or disintegrated me. But because the particles had mingled with dark matter . . ."

Gil paused, so I finished the thought.

"They destabilized the electron bonds within the atoms inside your body, allowing them all to move independently at the speed of near light, just as Dr. Klaus Nillsen theorized on day six of Geneva. Although he was speaking of galactic formation, not people."

Gil turned to Margie. "I finally have someone to talk to. This is great!"

I won't bore you with all the details—I feel confident saying you would be bored by all the details unless you plan on being an astrophysicist—but basically Gil explained the molecules in his body are held together by his consciousness. He's essentially made of pure energy. So, by concentrating, he can shoot force beams, move at a speed that is almost invisible to the human eye, and even rearrange his atoms to look like he's wearing a cable company uniform or a sweater vest when, in fact, he hasn't worn a stitch of clothing since the accident in the lab.

I started thinking that it would make for a pretty cool backstory in a comic book. But then I realized there was a question I hadn't asked.

"Who are *they*? You guys keep saying *they* changed the story of how you came to Earth in the comic books or *they* haven't decided if you even get a comic. Who are *they*?"

Both Gil and Margie got really quiet, and I could tell they were not sure if they should answer. But finally, Margie sighed.

"We're going to have to bring him in anyway."

Gil nodded, but not in a happy agreement way.

"You're right. Tell him."

Margie took a small breath, holding it a moment before she spoke.

"They . . . are MASC."

So now it was my turn to be confused. If she had said "masked," it wouldn't have made much sense either, but at least it would have been proper English. My confusion must have been obvious.

"It's really hard to . . . it's like . . . you just need to see for yourself."

11:51 P.M.
WEDNESDAY, OCTOBER 6

Gil propelled Margie and me up the 405 and then toward downtown LA on the 10 at speeds three times faster than any car on the road. Each time he'd pull his molecules together to push us along and then race ahead to catch us and push us again, it was like a mini whiplash— not quite as sudden as when we were fleeing Seismyxer but still not the most comfortable way to travel. Margie didn't seem affected by all the rapid accelerations. I couldn't tell if that was because of her alien constitution, or if she was just used to Gil's driving since they were married.

All I knew was it was well past my usual bedtime and I felt like I'd lost a fight with a carnival ride by the time we arrived at Hollywood Boulevard. I couldn't help noticing that even if anyone had seen my foster parents dressed as superheroes, they wouldn't have seemed all that out of place. There were enough people wearing colorful and skintight outfits on the street that Gil felt comfortable stopping in a dark doorway, putting us down, and letting us walk to our destination . . . which wasn't what I was expecting.

"Monolith Studios?"

That was me. I was totally baffled as we stood at the gates of one of Hollywood's oldest studios. It was strange because even though I'd lived in the Los Angeles area for almost a decade, I'd never been inside any of the movie studios. It isn't really something that locals do, except when they have visitors in from other states, and I'd never had a visitor.

"We're here for the studio tour," Margie said meaningfully to the thick-necked guard working the gate.

"Confirmation number?"

He spoke without looking up from his clipboard and I remember thinking he looked more like Navy SEAL than a security guard.

Margie responded, "One-four-three-six-one-six-eight-one-two-one."

It was all very strange. I knew that Monolith Studios only offered tours from 10 a.m. until 5 p.m. on weekdays. Also, they didn't take reservations. It was a first-come, first-served situation. These were both facts. It was on the board above the guard's head right there at the entrance. However, instead of telling Margie either of these facts, the guard punched the numbers into a keypad and asked Margie to look into a small webcam. A moment later, the gate went up and we were escorted inside, where we boarded a small tram pulled by a golf cart.

Gil leaned over and whispered to me.

"I know you must have a million questions . . . I mean . . . a million *more* questions. But if you ask questions, the guards . . . well, they might ask questions . . . so just pretend like you've done this before. Okay?"

You should know I'm not awesome at pretending. It's a form of lying. I tend to be better at speaking facts rather than things that are *not facts*. But I had enough information to act like this was not my first time on a studio tour. I'd read several dozen reviews of the Monolith tour online. I didn't expect much. It was not one of the higher-rated tours in town.

We were supposed to visit a sound stage where three of the top-ten-grossing movies ever were shot. Next, we'd get to visit the studio's monster makeup lab where one of us would get turned into an alien, which could have been interesting since one of us already was an alien. Then, our tour guide was supposed to take us to a screening room to see movie trailers.

None of that happened.

Instead, the tram went zooming around the lot for a few minutes and then headed straight for a three-story building. Now, when I say "headed straight" for the building, I mean we were heading directly at a building that had no garage door or loading dock. And yet the driver was accelerating. I was about to scream, which seemed a reasonable reaction to certain death, when I heard Margie's voice in my head.

Don't scream. You've been here before.

I managed to hold in my scream, and somehow we didn't die. Instead, we went right through the wall, which turned out to be a hologram. The tram cruised down a spiral road, like a corkscrew attached to the inside of a silo that had been built upside down. I figure we must've been down about fifty feet when it flattened out and our tram came to a stop in a high-tech underground parking lot filled with other trams, all facing a massive door. It looked like a bank vault door on steroids, at least twenty feet high and ten feet wide, made of a metal I couldn't identify. And there, on the door, were four stenciled letters.

MASC.

I tried to whisper. I really did. But I was super curious. "Can you tell me now: What's MASC?"

That's when several dozen soldiers in faded gray camo emerged from behind all the parked trams. They had weapons that I'd never seen before, all trained on us. I quickly realized this wasn't a standard greeting for Margie and Gil, because they suddenly went into a defensive posture, shielding me. I waited, eyes shut, bracing myself for the sound of gunshots or searing heat of laser beams, but instead, I heard a man's booming voice, thick with a Texas-sized southern twang.

"MASC is the Multinational Authority for Super-human Control!" The words echoed off the walls. "Quicksilver Siren and Ultra-Quantum, authenticate immediately."

I turned and saw that the massive door had opened and an older soldier in a fancy uniform was standing at the entrance. It was camo patterned, but burgundy colored. I couldn't imagine what terrain it would've been advantageous for, other than a Vegas casino. He had a bald head that sloped into a thick neck and broad shoulders. It all matched the way his barrel chest blended right into his round gut. But the thing I really noticed was the cigar in his mouth. You just don't see people smoking indoors much these days. Of course, that's because according to the Centers for Disease Control and Prevention's website, California is one of twenty-seven states that have laws making sure all workplaces, bars, and restaurants are smoke-free.

Margie saw the cigar guy at the same time but seemed unconcerned about his smoking.

"Colonel Gdula! What is going on? Tell your men to stand down!"

The colonel grinned sourly, like he'd only just realized he had a bunch of dried, burning leaves in his mouth.

"I don't take orders, *Margie* . . . I give them. Authenticate immediately."

Margie snarled and her skin turned silver all on its own. That was not something that happened in the comic books, but I was quickly realizing that the comic books did not include all the facts.

I thought for sure we were in for a firefight. As the only person in the room who did not have either superpowers or body armor, I was not happy about it. But then I heard Gil's voice. Not his superheroish voice, but the one he used most of the time.

"Dr. Quantum . . . no, Ultra-Quantum. S.I., Gil Grant. Authentication number five-zero-eight-eight-two-eight-five-six-zero-zero."

A robotic voice came over a loudspeaker.

"Authentication confirmed."

Gil looked at Margie meaningfully. I didn't really get what the meaning was at the time, but it must have convinced Margie to cooperate.

"Quicksilver Siren. S.I., Margie Morrow. Authentication number one-four-three-six-one-six-eight-one-two-one."

"Authentication confirmed."

The computer voice seemed satisfied, but the soldiers didn't lower their guns.

"Colonel . . . we . . . we just authenticated . . ."

Gil couldn't even finish his sentence, but Margie had no such issues.

"Somebody better explain what's going on or this is getting real ugly real fast!"

No one was saying anything, but everyone was acting really tough. In my experience, nothing good results from this behavior. I was about to say so when another voice spoke up. It was softer and older and came from a small, ancient-looking man with unkempt gray hair and a white lab coat that was about two inches too long.

"Colonel Gdula is worried you've been turned, my dear. And bringing an unexpected young guest with you isn't exactly helping your cause."

Suddenly, it felt like all eyes, and guns for that matter, were on me.

"It's not what you think . . ." was all Gil could muster.

Colonel Gdula's voice turned our heads again. "I am not interested in what anyone thinks! I'm only concerned with what I know, and I do not know that boy. You will surrender the unsecured adolescent immediately so we can run a threat assessment profile."

Margie held me tighter. It hurt, but for some reason it still felt like a better option than going with the soldiers.

"He's not a threat!" Margie exhaled. "He's our son."

12:17 A.M.
THURSDAY, OCTOBER 7

After Colonel Gdula picked his cigar off the floor and patted out the small burned spot where the embers had stuck to the front of his burgundy camo jacket, the guns were put away. Most of the security team went back to wherever they spend their time when they're not getting ready to open fire on two superheroes and their foster kid. Everyone had a lot of questions, which meant no one was willing to answer *my* questions.

"You want to tell me why you two have barely reported in for the past three weeks? You didn't reply to texts. You ignored calls. We went to the address we have on file for you and it was empty. Cleaned out!"

That was Gdula, standing in front of Gil and Margie with his arms crossed. Margie crossed her arms right back at him, leaving Gil to do the talking.

"We moved . . . out. To a place with room for Logan . . . And we needed a little . . . you know . . . family time."

Colonel Gdula listened, shook his head, and relit his now slightly bent cigar.

"You do realize we're in the middle of a threat-level-crimson crisis, don't you? Seismyxer's quakes have claimed over thirty civilians' lives, plus we've had six heroes eliminated in the line of duty and another two just went missing."

Margie's expression shifted when Gdula shared that information.

"Which two?"

Gdula grunted. "Quarry Lord has been gone for two weeks and FemmeFlorance disappeared a few days ago. We thought you two were in the same situation until about five minutes ago, so you'll pardon me for being a bit suspicious. There is a mole somewhere in this organization! I'm trying to figure out who it is while also keeping the western half of the United States safe. And you two decided to run off and play house? This is unacceptable!"

From the way most of the soldiers in the room winced when he yelled, I got the feeling that Colonel Gdula found many things unacceptable. However, the man in the lab coat seemed unfazed and was more curious about how it was possible that Gil and Margie had a child, what with her being an alien and him being a sentient mass of energy.

"I'm not their biological child," I explained. "I'm their foster child. I was going to point that out when Margie said I was their son, but I'm working on not interrupting people . . . plus there were a lot of guns aimed at us."

The elderly scientist nodded as if he understood, at which point, I was approached by the security soldiers who asked me a few questions and performed a full body search where they confiscated my flip phone. Then we were brought inside the facility where a MASC technician in a blue uniform sat down at a computer terminal and quickly accessed the supposedly confidential files at ESTO to confirm that I had, in fact, been placed with Margie Morrow and Gil Grant.

I figured that would make everything better, but instead, Colonel Gdula insisted Margie and Gil come with him to a debriefing room immediately.

"I want you two to account for every day since you went incommunicado, all the way up to this attack at the movie theater, which we now have to clean up!"

The doors slammed behind them and I was left standing alone in one of those crazy-long subterranean hallways you always see in movies about supersecret government agencies. That made me wonder whether the hall I was in was designed to look like the movies, or if the movies were actually designed to look like this place. After all, I was standing five stories under one of the biggest movie studios in Hollywood. I was just about to start inspecting the hallway more closely when the old guy in the lab coat came back out of the debriefing room.

"They'll be in there awhile. Why don't I give you a tour while you wait?"

It turns out his name was Dr. Francis X. Chrysler and he was the top scientist at the MASC laboratory. He took me all over the facility and showed me everything: the lab, barracks, the computer servers in a room protected by an invisible electromagnetic wall that cannot be penetrated by anything less than the force of a black hole. He even showed me part of the particle collider that stretches under Hollywood Boulevard all the way to Disneyland and back.

"MASC itself is only about a century old, but there have always been individuals on this planet with unusual abilities and powers," Dr. Chrysler explained. "Thousands of years ago, people called them demigods, heroes, angels, and messiahs . . . or wizards. Some were even labeled demons if they used their uniqueness to harm instead of help. Many became rulers. Kings and queens who claimed to be given power by God. Great leaders and notorious legends whose names you probably know."

And then he listed off pretty much every important

name in human history—Cleopatra, Nero, Hua Mulan, Attila the Hun, Galahad, Vlad the Impaler, Rasputin, and even Paul Bunyan—but his list ended about two hundred years ago. So I asked why.

"Earth, it was a simpler place until then," Dr. Chrysler explained. "News traveled slowly. There were no pictures or videos. It was harder to tell the difference between a tall tale and the truth. A person with superpowers could do a great deed and it wasn't like everyone would instantly know about it. But then along came photographs and telegraphs. Then radio, television, the internet now. As soon as technology appeared, these powerful individuals started to disappear. They had to."

Those were his words. To be clear, these powerful individuals didn't actually disappear, except for the ones who were able to turn invisible. Dr. Chrysler was being metaphorical.

"They all had to keep a lower profile. Some hid their powers entirely, living intentionally average lives. Most were afraid that they'd be persecuted and maybe even attacked if people knew what they could do.

"Then in 1918, after the end of World War One, the governments of the world met in secret and agreed that the human race needed heroes again. They convinced a few superpowered individuals to emerge from the shadows and band together with the world's leaders to form the

Multinational Authority for Superhuman Coordination— MASC."

"I thought the *C* stood for *Control*," I interjected. "That's what the colonel said."

"You noticed that, did you? Quite right, but originally it was for *Coordination*, because it started out as a partnership, based on a simple bargain: the superhumans agreed to be superheroes and be coordinated by us mere mortals in exchange for MASC giving each of them new names, birth certificates, school records, passports. We gave them secret identities that allowed them to live normal lives most of the time."

As we strolled down long corridor after long corridor, Dr. Chrysler went on to explain how after the original agreement was made, the founders reached out across the globe to find more superhumans who were willing to be heroes. Each nation had their own list, and MASC put it all together.

"A global network of superheroes, managed, regulated, and kept hidden by the greatest, most covert global alliance the planet has ever seen. And no one else on Earth needed to know about it . . . at least, that was the original goal," Dr. Chrysler explained as he walked me into the MASC cafeteria for breakfast.

I ordered French toast, and while we waited, I asked the obvious question.

"You said that *was* the goal. What changed?"

"Within twenty years of MASC's formation, the world was on the brink of another great war, and although MASC tried to defuse the situation, the Nazis made that impossible. They started recruiting rogue, superpowered individuals who were willing to fight—and even kill—in exchange for money, power, or other personal gains."

"Villains?" I asked.

Dr. Chrysler shrugged. "I don't like that term. I'm sure Colonel Gdula is happy to throw the label around, although I've found no one is a villain from his or her own point of view. But it's fair to say these superhumans had no inclination toward heroism. Some were mercenaries. Others were anarchists who enjoyed seeing the world tremble in fear. And one . . . she was different."

Dr. Chrysler paused for a moment, like he was thinking, but then our breakfast was ready so we took our trays and sat down to eat. (And, by the way, should you ever get a chance to try it, the MASC cafeteria makes the best French toast I've ever tasted. That's a fact.)

Between bites of his English muffin and sips of tea, Dr. Chrysler continued. "At that point, with the Nazis amassing their own superhuman forces to take onto the battlefield, MASC couldn't stay on the sidelines any longer. Remaining neutral would have led to fascist world domination. But we also knew it would be impossible to keep the superheroes' existence secret much longer, especially if they were going to be in combat. The solution was . . . comic books."

I was confused, because I knew that certain kinds of comic books had existed for almost half a century before World War Two. So I told him, "I'm confused, because certain kinds of comic books existed for almost half a century before World War Two."

"Indeed. However, up until then, comic books were . . . comic. They were about frivolous things, meant to elicit laughs from children. But the medium was ideal for making impossible things seem possible. It was the perfect way to introduce the world to great heroes while blurring the lines between what was real and what was imagined. Most of all, it made these superhuman individuals familiar so that on the very rare occasion when a civilian saw one of them in action, they'd assume they were seeing someone *dressed like* a superhero, rather than the genuine article. And it worked. First it was just the comic books. Then it was radio shows, followed by movies, television, video games, and now online videos. In the past eighty years, MASC has given the world literally millions of hours of entertainment and funded its own operations around the world with the royalties, all while keeping the planet safe."

"But that doesn't make sense," I pointed out. "Why aren't the superhumans running things if they're the ones that have the powers?"

Dr. Chrysler smiled for a second, but then the smile faded. "Have you ever noticed that in most countries, there is a military that has all the firepower, and then there's a government that runs the m itary, even though they don't have any firepower of their own?"

I nodded but pointed out, "Except in places where there have been military coups like Burundi in 1996 and Pakistan in 1999 and—"

"Yes, exactly. The point is there's a danger in giving a group that already has firepower . . . too much power. That's why it was decided the superheroes needed oversight. And since there are eight billion people on the planet who have no superpowers and only a few thousand who do, unless the superhumans want to stage a super revolution where they would be outnumbered a million to one . . ."

Dr. Chrysler never actually concluded the sentence. He just let it hang in the air, but I got it. The idea of humanity going to war with a bunch of superhumans didn't sound great for either side.

We finished our breakfasts and were about to walk out of the cafeteria when a chiseled, imposing man walked in wearing a mask that wrapped around his nose and mouth and a full-body, skintight aqua wet suit made out of some fabric that looked more liquid than solid. I recognized him immediately from the comics.

"You're TideStrider! You can control all forms of water

with your mind and speak to aquatic creatures and create tsunamis and—"

Dr. Chrysler put his hand on my shoulder, which stopped me but also made me pull away involuntarily.

"Sorry, Yuhei, the boy is getting the tour. Enjoy your breakfast."

TideStrider nodded. "Gotta fuel up. I'm going out looking for Luther and Genevieve on my patrol."

Dr. Chrysler raised his eyebrows. "Quarry Lord and FemmeFlorance, yes . . . good. We can't have heroes disappearing like this. Very concerning. Come see me before you go. I may have an idea about where you should start looking."

Then the tour continued, with Dr. Chrysler showing me around the lower level of the sprawling subterranean base, but my brief introduction to TideStrider had given me a whole new batch of questions.

"So every superhero I've ever read about is real?" I asked. It seemed a reasonable assumption given what I'd seen, but Dr. Chrysler chuckled and shook his head.

"Not at all. Some are total fabrications. And for the record, all the archenemies you've read about are fictional. No purpose giving the real ones free publicity."

"But there are vill—I mean—archenemies? Like bad guys with superpowers that you all fight against?"

"Oh, certainly. There have always been some

superhumans whose goals or powers were not aligned with MASC. Over the years, we've captured several and battled others. But the most dangerous and most persistent one is called Necros. She has the ability to siphon life energy from anyone or anything she touches and use it to heal or strengthen herself. It has allowed her to stay alive for centuries, though we aren't sure exactly how many. She may have been born in ancient Egypt, or possibly during the Black Death in Europe. For that matter, she may have actually been the Black Death . . . we just don't know."

I think I was terrified hearing this because I felt some sweat trickle down my back. But I know for sure I was also curious. "So if she wants to, she can kill with a single touch?"

"It's not a matter of whether she wants to. Her touch is death . . . and as far as our research has shown, no living creature is immune. Can you imagine that kind of power . . . and the darkness that comes with it? There is so much we don't know about her, but one thing is certain: even from the earliest days of MASC, long before I arrived, she hated the authority. When the Nazis approached her in 1942, she offered to join the Axis powers in exchange for the eradication of MASC once they won."

"But that's not what happened," I pointed out. "The Allies won the war."

Dr. Chrysler nodded and got a faraway look.

"That's right. The Axis was defeated with MASC's help. Necros escaped and disappeared in the aftermath; and in the months and years following, superheroes became big business. So the need to control them became more urgent. When a new, potentially marketable hero emerges, we slip him or her into the comic books; change a few of their powers so MASC's enemies can't know for sure what they're capable of; and off we go, making money and saving the planet all over again without anyone ever knowing."

"But why bother with it at all? Why not just let everyone know the truth?"

"It could start a panic. Like I said, humanity needs to feel like it's at the top of the food chain. If everyone knew there were individuals with superpowers among them, they might feel scared or threatened. Besides, there's the public pool paradox to consider."

I'd never heard of the public pool paradox. Dr. Chrysler explained the reason for that.

"That's because I was the one who created it. Here's how it goes: You're at a public pool and you notice that a small child has swum into the deep end and started to drown. What do you do?"

I explained to him that I never went in public pools and listed off eleven different infections one can contract from public bathing, including hepatitis A and hemorrhagic jaundice.

"Okay, so hypothetically . . . what would you do if you were assured that the pool was sanitary?"

I thought about the question and answered honestly.

"I'd alert the lifeguard. According to Title twenty-two, Division four of the California Code of Regulations they have to maintain continuous surveillance of the pool users."

The aged scientist nodded and smiled.

"Nine out of ten respondents give that answer . . . although you're the only one to ever cite the actual code. But what if the lifeguard didn't respond right away? Maybe she didn't hear you, or she was distracted."

"I'd yell louder. I'd wave my arms. I'd make sure she heard."

"Indeed. And then, if she still didn't jump in the water?"

"I am not a strong swimmer, but I guess I'd try to save the child myself if the lifeguard wasn't going to do it."

Dr. Chrysler held his hands out to his side.

"And if by the time you got to the child, it was too late . . . who would you say was at fault?"

It was an easy question, so I answered quickly.

"The lifeguard. She didn't do her job."

"Now what if you were in that same pool, and you saw the same kid go under, and you knew there was no lifeguard on duty? What would you do then?"

I didn't answer because I saw the point right away.

"It's like the studies John Darley and Bibb Latané did in 1968 where they defined the bystander effect," I pointed out, drawing an enthusiastic agreement from Dr. Chrysler.

"Exactly. The diffusion of responsibility. People are capable of solving most problems on their own if they think it's their problem to solve. But if they think someone else could have solved it, humans are quick to point fingers. First responders, soldiers, doctors—they all are targeted for blame if something goes wrong on their watch . . . and those are just ordinary people. Can you imagine if everyone knew there were superheroes out there? You'd have billions of people waiting to be saved and blaming superhumans every time they weren't. Who would ever want to be a superhero in that world?"

I didn't have an answer. I knew I wouldn't want to be hero like that, but, then again, I never wanted to be a hero in the first place.

Dr. Chrysler's tour continued, and I saw a training gym with thousand-pound barbells and treadmills that went up to two hundred miles per hour. The coolest area was the holographic shooting range with titanium walls. The weird thing was, there was no one using any of the equipment. Then I remembered hearing about all the heroes going missing lately, which got me thinking.

"How come there haven't been more rumors about heroes being real?"

"The human mind is happy to accept a semi-reasonable lie much more readily than an inconvenient fact. If a person sees a man with cool tattoos and a trident jump out of the ocean, it's much easier to believe they're seeing someone cosplaying rather than accept that they actually just saw the real Aquaman."

"And that works every time?"

"Not *every time* . . . we do have a fallback plan, just in case."

5:19 A.M.
THURSDAY, OCTOBER 7

I probably should have said this earlier, but in case you hadn't figured it out yet . . . you can't tell anyone anything about superheroes or supervillains or any of it. If you're like me, you don't like being told what you can and cannot say. But I want to keep you out of trouble, and MASC definitely doesn't play around when it comes to keeping secrets.

Dr. Chrysler got a little twinkle in his eye as he ushered me into a room where there were a half-dozen chairs like the ones you'd see in a dentist's office, but with a headpiece that reminded me of the enormous hair dryers they use on women in old-time beauty salons.

"What are these things?"

"This technology was actually something I developed by working with Harry Houdini."

I'd read all about Houdini, including one book by William Kalush and Larry Sloman called *The Secret Life of Harry Houdini: The Making of America's First Superhero*. It makes no mention of MASC.

"Did you ever wonder how Houdini did so many amazing tricks and stunts? Harry's gift was the ability to erase and replace memories: a form of mass hypnosis. He'd stand onstage, tell everyone he was about to do something impossible, and then put the whammy on them . . . hundreds, even thousands at a time. . . . They'd walk away, sure they had witnessed him escape from chains or a guillotine. Everyone knew it was a trick. But the real trick was that he never actually did the trick. When I came on board in the late thirties, my first project was working with him to transfer his powers—"

"That can't be right," I interrupted. "Harry Houdini died on Halloween of 1926."

Dr. Chrysler went to put his hand on my shoulder again and I must have winced, because he pulled his hand back with an apology. "Sorry, Logan . . . but if we can keep a lid on the existence of a massive organization that coordinates hundreds of superheroes all over the planet, don't you think we can handle fudging the death of one magician?"

It was a valid point.

"Houdini was already one of the most famous men on the planet when he was recruited by MASC. But we couldn't just give him a secret identity and send him out to save the world with a mask. We had to take him out of circulation for a while, so MASC staged his death. And it was more than a decade later that I was the first one to replicate the energy his brain emitted to erase people's memories." Dr. Chrysler gestured to the room full of techy recliners. "These are my Time-Sensitive Neurocognitive Manipulation Apparatuses . . . but we just call them Houdini chairs. They are a last resort for when someone has seen something we can't explain away."

"So you can wipe away memories and then put in new ones?" I asked.

"Only half right, Logan. We can erase memories, but we can't replace them. That was a trick Houdini took to his grave . . . in 1955 for the record. Whenever you hear about someone who has amnesia or can't remember the car accident they survived . . . there's a good chance that might be us."

As someone who remembers everything, I wasn't overjoyed to learn that someone had invented a way to erase memories. But by then, the tour was just about over. I still got to see the containment cells where they keep rogue superhumans, the restrooms (it had been over nine hours since I went at the movie theater), and an entire hallway full of escape pods. When you have a secret facility with a particle collider and superpowered individuals walking/ flying through the doors every day, it's a good idea to have a safe evacuation plan.

Finally, we ended up in the master control room. It looked like NASA. Hundreds of flat-screen monitors on walls, workstations manned by a bunch of people who might have looked nerdier than I do, and more computers than I've ever seen in one place.

"This is where we monitor and regulate all super-human activity west of the Mississippi River, Logan. Some are scanning social media to see if there are situations that require I.S.I.—immediate superhero intervention—while others are updating the master database with information we've collected. That's really the most valuable asset we have. Our database keeps track of all the powers, weaknesses, and secret identities of every known and suspected superhuman on Earth. The good guys . . . the not so good guys. For example, we recently uploaded information on that fellow your foster parents fought, Seismyxer. He's new, but he's already one of the most lethal threats in the database. He's been linked to a half-dozen hero deaths in the past few months, and countless innocents have been hurt in his attacks. It's awful, really. . . ."

Dr. Chrysler paused and looked shaken. Or maybe he just forgot what he was going to say next.

Because I can't help but consider possibilities, I spoke up.

"It sounds like he either really dislikes MASC or really enjoys killing."

The thought seemed to bring Dr. Chrysler back into focus. "I'm afraid it may be both. He wasn't born with his powers . . . at least we don't believe so because there's no evidence of him having them until last year. It appears he can manipulate existing seismic energy, though he can't make it out of nothing. We think that's why he sticks to places like Southern California, where fault lines are plentiful. We're acquiring data like that all the time, but it's information so sensitive that no one here, not even me, can access the entire database. The information is relayed from one randomly selected MASC facility to another every four and a half minutes. I don't mean to brag . . . again . . . but I developed the fail-safe myself. As soon as the full file is downloaded, it's updated and immediately gets sent to another random facility, so it's never all in one place for more than a second or two."

"What's the point of having all the information and not being able to use it?" I asked.

"We use it, Logan. But these terminals only allow us to search for specific names, locations, or powers. The user only gets data results that match their search. No one ever has all the information at their disposal, because if all that information fell into the wrong hands, the very survival of

MASC, and every one of the superheroes we work with, would be in danger."

I guess I must have looked confused, because he felt the need to elaborate.

"It's like writing down your ATM PIN, your email password, your Apple ID, and your social security number all on one piece of paper that you keep in your pocket. Sure, you'll never forget the numbers, but it also means that if anyone ever picks your pocket, they can take everything."

I explained that I'd never write those things down on a piece of paper because of my eidetic memory. That perked the old scientist up quite a bit. For a minute, I thought he was going to take me into the lab and study my brain, which might have been cool. I've always wondered how it works too. But before he got the chance, Colonel Gdula barged through the door with Gil and Margie.

"We've got a bad news, good news scenario, Doc. On the negative side, Quicksilver Siren and Ultra-Quantum broke protocol in about a dozen different ways. They moved their place of residence, failed to check in regularly for the past three weeks, and apparently used their secret identities to acquire a foster child and bring him here. Under the regulations they agreed to when they signed on with MASC, both of them should be facing indefinite suspension. However, I've told them I'm willing to suspend their suspensions since we are at DEFCON One and most of our West Coast operatives are MIA or worse. Our intel says Necros is behind it all and ramping up for something even bigger. We need every able-bodied asset in the field or the death toll could be in the thousands."

It sounded pretty grim when he put it all together like that.

"You said there was good news, Colonel?" Dr. Chrysler asked patiently.

"As far as I can tell, neither of them has been compromised by Necros. Also, the boy checks out as just a civilian, rather than a spy. So we can just put him in a chair, wipe the past three or four weeks away, and send him back to the orphanage."

5:47 A.M.
THURSDAY, OCTOBER 7

After my long, leisurely tour through MASC HQ, suddenly, everything was happening all at once. Margie got right in the colonel's face and little bits of silver formed at the corners of her mouth. She was shouting about what she would do to him if he tried to take me and it sounded pretty unpleasant. He was hollering back at her about the chain of command and insubordination. Gil pleaded with Dr. Chrysler and warned him about the effects of a Houdini chair on a mind like mine. I got the feeling Dr. Chrysler didn't disagree, but he also didn't seem all that averse to giving it a try. There were also all the technicians and security commandos in the room, asking everyone to calm down.

And then there was me. I felt myself sweating through the armpits of my shirt, rubbing my eyes, and simultaneously reciting the names, in alphabetical order, on the Stanley Cup.

"Clarence Abel, Sid Abel, Douglas Acer, Keith Acton, Craig Adams, Jack Adams, John M. Adams, Kevyn Adams—"

That's when the sirens began blaring as the largest monitor in the room lit up with a message: "Incoming Transmission." Then the monitor filled up with a long, continuous scroll of data and a small digital clock in the corner that immediately started counting down from 270.

For a moment, all the shouting stopped. The colonel's eyes widened and he bit clean through his cigar. Dr. Chrysler turned pale, looked at his watch, and pressed a glowing red button by the door.

"We must clear the room of anyone without level-eight clearance," Dr. Chrysler announced.

That's when the confusion turned to chaos. The security team drew their weapons once again. Margie's skin went full silver and Gil instantly flashed into action, deactivating each gun milliseconds before the soldiers could pull their triggers. And there was so much noise. Everyone started shouting at each other to leave or not move or stand down. I can't tell you everything that was said because between the sirens and the yelling it kind of overloaded my ability to process it all and I just covered my ears with my hands.

Colonel Gdula mouthed a curse word and hit a different, but equally red, button. More commandos appeared, this time through a door behind me. Two of the security soldiers grabbed my arms and started dragging me out. I figured it was the last time I'd see Gil and Margie; but before I got to the door, Gil flashed into sight, swiped me from the guards, and whisked me up to a catwalk above the control room.

"Stay here! I'll come back once we can get you out. Okay?" And then he was gone in a blink of light.

I could see the entire fight from up high. Margie knocked fully armed soldiers around like they were action figures. Gil took out an entire battalion before they could even aim to fire. Colonel Gdula shouted orders as Dr. Chrysler ran out the door. The whole time, that one big screen scrolled with data.

It was bedlam. That is a fact. And that was before the rumbling started.

At first, no one below noticed the ground shaking—but I knew exactly what it was, because I'd felt it the night before.

I shouted to Gil and Margie, but they couldn't hear me.

I had no choice. I found the nearest ladder and scrambled down toward the battle. I was the only one who could warn them, but I hadn't even made it halfway when the rumbling turned into something bigger. A pounding. Like Godzilla—who, until now, I had no reason to believe could be a real thing—was trying to tell a knock-knock joke.

Seismyxer exploded through the far wall of the control room, sending hunks of concrete and cinder blocks flying everywhere.

"Well, look who's here. I thought I gotten rid of you two at the movies. . . . Guess this is the sequel!"

Seismyxer glared at my foster parents. The air around him started rippling with power.

Colonel Gdula ordered his troops to stop Seismyxer, and the commandos turned and opened fire on the intruder. Their guns shot these mondo-powerful pulses of magnetic plasma. I figured this out the hard way because one of the blasts missed Seismyxer and plastered me against the wall next to the ladder. It hurt like crazy but didn't obliterate me like I thought it would. Instead, I found myself stuck to concrete about ten feet off the ground, like a kid's drawing being held up by a fridge magnet.

And yet the weapons weren't having any effect on Seismyxer. He had these metal bands around his wrists that absorbed the blasts. But whenever the shots missed him, the balls of plasma slammed into the wall behind him, which was where I was. Margie saw it from across the room and barreled into the commandos to keep them from firing again.

"Stop shooting! You're going to kill him!"

I appreciated the help. But apparently Colonel Gdula

misunderstood which *him* Margie meant and thought she was protecting Seismyxer.

"Traitors! I knew it!" Colonel Gdula erupted at Gil and Margie. "They're working together!" he shouted to his troops. "You are authorized to use full lethal force on all of them! Now!"

The soldiers flicked the switches on their weapons.

When the first soldier got a shot off, a different kind of force bolt exploded out of his gun. Seismyxer's wristbands didn't absorb it this time. They deflected it instead, and the ricochet blew a hole in the ceiling the size of a large pizza. The soldiers seemed as stunned by the force of the blast as anyone, but then Colonel Gdula yelled at his men to fire and everyone started blasting away. In less than a minute, the room was full of pizza-sized holes. One of the blasts slammed into the main monitor exactly 3.21 seconds before the countdown clock got to zero. The computer exploded in a shower of sparks.

That's when Seismyxer went nuts.

"You . . . are all . . . dead!" he bellowed, sending out shock waves that were strong enough to knock the soldiers off their feet and to unpin me from the wall. I might have really hurt myself falling the ten feet to the floor, but fortunately I landed on a technician.

Before I had a chance to thank him for cushioning my fall, I was moving at blur speed again. Gil whisked me

out of the control room as Margie shielded our exit with a massive metal desk. Stray blasts and seismic waves bounced all around us.

"Now what?" Gil asked Margie as he flashed up and down the various hallways.

"We have to get out of here!" Margie said, stating the obvious.

That's when I found myself playing the role of tour guide.

"Down here," I told them, motioning to an empty hallway that led deeper into the base.

To their credit, Gil and Margie didn't argue. They just followed my directions past the gym, through a set of doors, past the labs filled with glowing tubes and massive computers, as the hallways behind us filled with soldiers. Before long, we'd made our way to a row of escape pods.

"I forgot these were even here," Margie admitted. "Let's go!"

Gil protested. "We can get Logan to safety, but then we have to come back."

I've seen a lot of foster parents argue with each other over the years, and I'm pretty used to being the cause of it all. But this was different. This time there was no time. So while they bickered, I slipped into the nearest escape pod, slid the door closed, and hit the launch button.

The pod shot up for a few seconds, then ejected me,

and I tumbled out of a dumpster, landing roughly in an abandoned alley just off Hollywood Boulevard. I've been thrown *into* dumpsters before, but never *out* of one.

I was a bit unsteady. I'm not a fan of thrill rides, and it felt like I'd just come off the world's least-fun roller coaster. Dawn was breaking as I made my way out to the main street and peeked around the corner. Smoke rose into the air from a few blocks away, in the general direction of Monolith Studios. The ground was still thrumming with tremors. The people out at that hour were all running for safety as another massive shock wave crumbled the last standing studio buildings in the distance.

After a beat, I saw someone . . . or multiple some-ones . . . flying up from the dust cloud and into the rising sun on a hoverboard. It was hard to make out details with the haze and sun, but I could tell Seismyxer had gotten away and had maybe taken a person with him.

"Logan!"

That was Gil and Margie. Margie's eyebrows were almost touching each other and she was doing the thing where you whisper really loudly, which I've been told can mean a person is angry.

"Get back over here!" Margie barked.

"Why did you take off?" Gil asked. "We hadn't decided what we were going to do yet!"

But I had decided what I was going to do, so I said, "I

know, but I had decided what I was going to do. I'm going back to ESTO. I can't stay with you guys; they'll never let me."

"Of course you can! We'll just . . ." Margie tried to protest, but it was Gil who understood.

"He's right, Margie. MASC won't allow it . . . and they think we've . . . you know . . . gone rogue, especially now. And Seismyxer keeps turning up when we're trying to have . . . um . . . family time. . . ."

Margie put her heel down so hard it cracked the pavement.

"No! I don't know if it's different here, but on my planet, a mother would never send her child away—especially if she was the only one who might be able to protect him. I'm sorry, Logan, but there is no one I trust besides us to keep you safe. Colonel Gdula is correct about one thing: there's a mole somewhere in MASC." Margie turned to Gil, who was slowly realizing she was right. "Someone's helping Seismyxer and now they know who Logan is. So far, there's only been one place no one has been able to find us. . . ."

"Home." Gil realized. "We never told anyone we moved . . . until today. But now it's in the database. . . ."

"I wouldn't be so sure about that."

That was me. Gil and Margie seemed surprised that I had an opinion on the matter.

"The database transfer got stopped before it completed. That was the big screen with the siren, right? Dr. Chrysler said it takes four and a half minutes to download before the new data is uploaded. The computer blew up before it finished, so our—I mean your—address should still be a secret."

There was a long pause.

"He's right." Gil admitted. "The house is still our safest bet."

By the same logic, I figured ESTO would be safe too, but it turned out that there was a detail I didn't know.

"Colonel Gdula ran a full background check, Logan. He insisted on knowing everything about you."

Suddenly, I wasn't worried about supervillains anymore.

"Does he know about my birth parents? Did he tell you where they are? Do I have a brother or a sister?"

All Gil and Margie knew was that the colonel said I had checked out.

"But if he ran that check, Logan," Gil explained, "there's a chance whoever is sharing information with Seismyxer and Necros will come looking for you at the orphanage."

"And eventually they'll find the house that same way," I completed the logic.

"So we have to work fast." Margie seemed resolved.

"We have to keep a low profile. And we have to find Seis-myxer and bring him in to the Nevada MASC facility."

"Is it Area Fifty-One?" I asked. I've read *Area 51: An Uncensored History of America's Top Secret Military Base* by Annie Jacobsen. Until that moment, I didn't think it had a lot of facts.

"Vegas, actually. Underneath the Vatican Hotel and Casino."

That would not have been my second guess.

"We can use Seismyxer as a bargaining chip so Logan can . . ." Margie paused and looked at me. "So Logan can have his life back. But we've got to get out of here."

That's when I noticed that MASC soldiers and techni-cians were emerging from other dumpsters that lined the alley, looking dazed, but alive. A wave of sirens headed our way.

"And remember. We've got to blend in."

Gil's body glimmered for a second, and suddenly he was in jeans and a T-shirt, but Margie was still stuck in her superhero gear with nothing to change into.

"I'll be back in a flash," Gil offered . . . and he was. He literally flashed away and was back a moment later with a pair of pink sweatpants that said *LA* in rhinestones across the butt and a purple Hollywood tank top.

"Sorry. The twenty-four-hour souvenir shop was the only place open."

6:59 A.M.
THURSDAY, OCTOBER 7

It is not a short or direct bus ride from Hollywood to Westchester. That is a fact. But having Gil streak us home in full daylight seemed unwise, especially with how many people were looking for us, and the time together on the 210 and 111 busses did give me a chance to ask Gil and Margie the question I'd been wondering about ever since I met them.

"Why did you guys pick me?"

The bus windows rattled as we rode over a pothole and then the brakes hissed gently in preparation for our next stop. Still, it felt like there was total silence. Margie and Gil looked to each other, but neither answered right away.

I realized it was possible they didn't have an answer . . . but it felt more like they just didn't want to say what they were thinking.

"There's a good chance I'll have my brain erased soon, so you should just tell the truth. Besides, you two are not very good liars, which is a little surprising, since you have secret identities."

It's strange to me that telling the truth makes so many people feel uncomfortable.

"We really want to be parents, Logan." Margie sighed. "On my planet, not all women are able to carry a child and those that can have a great responsibility. Our leaders dictate who marries who to ensure the strongest genetic code survives. I was lucky. My body grew strong and I was raised knowing that I would be able to be a mother . . . and always wanting to be one. But when the time came, I couldn't bring myself to just accept whoever the leadership decided would be my husband. I didn't want them to decide the fate of my body. So I enlisted in the Exploratory Force instead, assuming that the chance to be a mother would always be waiting for me. But then I got marooned on Earth when the wormhole collapsed, and the choice was taken out of my hands."

Gil put his arm around her.

"It's something we talked about for a long time," Gil explained. "I had an adopted brother growing up . . . so it made sense to me. But we knew it probably wasn't fair, to the child, I mean. It's not like we have normal jobs," Gil admitted. "It's dangerous . . . a lot of time superheroes have a *killer* retirement plan. . . . You know what I mean?"

Margie didn't wait to see if I got the pun—which I did. "We decided that the only way we could do it responsibly was to adopt someone who was old enough to take care of themself. And we wanted to find someone who was unlikely to find a placement elsewhere but who deserved a family. We know what it's like to feel different, so we thought we'd be the right parents for someone else who didn't exactly fit in either."

"Someone a bit like us . . ." Gil stammered. "Not superhuman or anything . . . just someone who wasn't . . . you know."

I took it all in and fed it back to them in much simpler terms.

"You wanted to find an unadoptable freak who might appreciate one last chance at having anyone to call mom and dad. Got it."

I don't know whether Gil and Margie disagreed with my summary of their answer, or if it was too accurate, but we didn't talk for the rest of the bus ride. That is a fact.

When we got back to the house, Gil and Margie had me stay outside while they made sure the house was safe. I didn't argue. It's pretty sensible to be cautious when a secret organization and at least one supervillain are hunting you.

While I was alone, I thought about why Gil and Margie had chosen me. On a logical level, I could appreciate their process. They were right: I wasn't going to find another set of foster parents who wanted to adopt me. But for some reason, the logic of it didn't make me feel better, which is odd. Usually, logic really helps.

"Nice hair, Logan."

Elena was coming out of the house on the right, dressed for school. She looked good. Apparently, I did not.

"Lemme guess. You just got out of bed and you're allergic to showers and hairbrushes, right?"

I informed her I'd never actually gotten into bed. She thought it was a joke. I didn't correct her.

"Do you need a ride? My mom can take us . . . unless you feel like riding the bus."

I'd had enough of buses for the day. I told her I had to run inside to see if I was going to school at all. Everything I said seemed to confuse Elena, but she agreed to wait.

Inside, I found Gil and Margie arguing. They didn't notice me at first.

"I'm not going to just send him back there, Gil! We knew this wouldn't be easy—"

"It's not about easy, Margie. What if . . . I mean, you heard Gdula. Necros is gearing up for something big . . .

and not good. What if he's safer there than here?"

"We're superheroes. If he's not safe with us . . ."

I cleared my throat. They both stopped at once and Margie kind of blushed a little. Gil didn't, but I don't think his body works that way anymore anyway.

"Am I going to school today? Elena offered me a ride."

Gil shot Margie a look.

"Might be the safest place . . . out in the public, and it'll give us time to put together . . . you know . . . likely hideouts for Seismyxer . . . see what *shakes* out."

Margie shook her head, though I couldn't tell if that was because of his plan or his pun.

"Logan, you have your phone. If anything goes—"

"I don't have my phone," I interrupted. "They took it away at MASC."

Margie exhaled, reached into her purse, and pulled out her smartphone.

"We're going to find Seismyxer and settle this. I promise. Until we do, take this with you. Don't answer it unless it's a call from Gil's mobile. Call us if you see anything or if you don't feel safe. And if it's a real emergency, use speed dial nine. It will alert MASC to your whereabouts and they'll send a tactical team. I know that probably doesn't seem like a great option right now, but if it's between that or Seismyxer . . . Do you need me to write any of this down?"

I just stared at her until she got it.

"Right. Photographic memory, What else? Oh . . . here. For lunch."

She handed me a twenty-dollar bill and then pulled a granola bar out of the cabinet. It's strange to admit now but watching her try to get me fed and off to school while also worrying about tracking down a superhuman villain was the first time where I felt like she could actually maybe be my mom. And that maybe, somehow, I could be her kid.

I started to leave, but before I got to the door, Margie called to me. When I turned, she walked over and took my hands in hers and held them tight. I considered pulling them away out of habit, but she really is very strong.

"Logan . . . what we said about why we picked you. It was true, but it wasn't everything. We both saw something in you—your honesty and the way you've taken care of yourself. We have powers, so people have made us feel *special* instead of just *strange*. But you . . . you've never had the benefit of that. You're still this amazing person. And you don't let other people's views on what's an ability or what's a disability define you. *You* define you. So, yes, we picked you for all the selfish reasons we said, but we also picked you because of who you are. We care about you. And we feel awful that we've put you in danger. That's not what parents do for their children. You deserve better."

Margie had tears in her eyes again. This time, I realized

her tears really were silvery. It wasn't just that they were reflecting a movie trailer.

Gil came over and put one hand on her shoulder and then looked at me.

"I . . . we . . . me too. I'm bad at this dad thing. Or I'm dad at this bad thing. But we just want you to be happy and safe."

I nodded and I think I smiled at them. I can't be sure, because when I've tried to smile in the mirror, just to practice, I think it looks more like I'm grimacing. Anyway, whether I smiled or grimaced, I knew they were telling the truth. I also knew why the logic of their original answer hadn't been enough for me. I had wanted a better answer—and I felt better now that I had finally gotten one.

4:14 P.M.
THURSDAY, OCTOBER 7

A piece of brotherly advice for you: never, under any circumstances, wear the same clothing to school two days in a row. Even if you wash them in between—just don't. I might be one of the few kids in the world with an eidetic memory, but it was amazing how many of my schoolmates immediately recognized that I'd worn exactly the same clothes the day before.

Most just made comments or laughed at me, but Jeff and Saul got the rest of the Hott Diarrhea Boys to spread a rumor that I was homeless. By lunchtime, they were taking up a collection in the quad, holding cans that read "Funds for Fartster." The oddest thing is that while they were doing it, I kept waiting for someone to swoop in to stop them. After spending the past twelve hours with my superhero foster parents, I'd fallen victim to my own personal public pool paradox.

At one point, a call came into Margie's phone, but I didn't recognize the number. I didn't answer it, in case it was MASC trying to track them down. Whoever it was didn't leave a message either, so it might have just been a telemarketer.

Around sixth period, an earthquake shook the clock off the wall in our Spanish class, and we had to evacuate. Outside on the athletic field, I found myself looking for Margie, even though I knew she was probably off chasing down Seismyxer. I realized that the big tremor might have meant she actually found him, or worse, that he had found the house. For the next several hours, I had this feeling in my stomach like it was tight and kind of jumpy. I realize now that I was nervous; but at the time, I worried I was suffering from the beginning stages of a burst appendix. According to HealthTap.com, about 2 percent of people with a burst appendix die from it. There are no reliable survival rates for people being hunted by supervillains.

I took the bus home, enduring another round of verbal abuse from Jeff and Saul's crew. Whenever we passed a thrift shop on the road, they begged the driver to pull over. "Please, Ms. Bus Lady! We've got a dollar and thirty cents. That's enough for Fartster to get a week's worth of used tighty-whities!" I didn't say a word about the fact that I actually wear boxers.

When I finally got off the bus, I was relieved to see the house was still standing. But once I went inside, it became clear that I was alone.

No Margie. No Gil. Just a note on the kitchen table.

Got a message from Dr. Chrysler. He gave us a lead about where to find Seismyxer and a chance to clear our names. Home for dinner, but left meat loaf in fridge in case.

I tried to wait. But it turns out I'm terrible at doing nothing. So I looked around for Gil's laptop, but it wasn't anywhere in the house. I even looked in the fridge. The computer wasn't there, but I did see that Margie had cooked up what I can only assume was an alien's approximation of meat loaf. I went outside and considered working on my bicycle riding, but I decided I'd already had a bad enough day. Instead, I sat down on the front steps, Margie's phone in my hand, and watched planes land, memorizing the call signs on the jets without meaning to.

Between planes, I watched a few of my favorite cat videos on Margie's phone, but for some reason, they didn't make me laugh for once. Turning the phone over in my hands a few times, I considered calling Gil's mobile, but they weren't even really late or anything. I also looked at the speed-dial list and checked out what the real number for Margie's 9 emergency call was. It was very long.

So I just kept watching planes. At about five, I saw Elena's dad, Arturo, leave his house. He's pretty much the exact opposite of Elena's mom. He's short; and for someone as short as me to say an adult is short, it must be true. But the guy is also big. His chest looks like an oil drum and his arms barely fit into the short-sleeved mechanic's shirt he was wearing. His hands are massive too. Elena always jokes that he's the only guy in the garage that can unscrew lug nuts with his fingers. He gave me a wave and hopped into a 1998 Mercedes sedan that looked like it just rolled off the factory floor.

I was still there an hour later when he returned with Elena. The sun was setting, and I hadn't heard from Gil or Margie.

"What's up, Logan?"

Elena bounced out of the car in her volleyball uniform and was beside me in barely a half-dozen steps.

"Just waiting for Gil and Margie to get home." I tried to say it as casually as possible, but since I really don't know what casual feels like, I guess I didn't get it right because Elena frowned.

"Everything okay? You could come over to our house if you didn't want to wait alone. Dad's making chicken chilaquiles for dinner. They're—"

"A Mexican baked casserole often served at brunch using lightly fried tortillas, green tomatillo salsa, onions, cilantro, and cheeses. At least according to FoodNetwork. com."

"Do you like them?"

I shrugged. I'd never had them before, so I went with her into the house on the left and stayed for dinner. And for the record, chilaquiles are delicious, and I think the reason they're served at brunch might be because people can't wait until later in the day to have them.

Still, dinner was a little odd for me. Elena and her dad seemed to know each other so well. There were a couple of times Elena finished her father's stories or prevented him from telling embarrassing ones about her. My foster parents have never seemed to know what I was going to say, or even understand it once I've said it. I assume that's because real families have known each other their whole lives, or maybe it goes beyond that.

Anyway, Elena caught me checking the phone every few minutes under the table, and as soon as we finished helping her father wash the dishes, she pulled me aside.

"You barely said anything during dinner. And you always say a lot more than barely anything."

"I just haven't heard from Gil or Margie. They left a note saying they'd be home around dinnertime. Of course, they didn't specify an actual time, so if they were thinking of a late dinner, it's possible . . ."

"Why don't you just call them?" The way Elena said it stopped me midsentence because I realized I didn't really have an answer. I didn't know if I was worried that I'd interrupt them in the middle of battling a supervillain or if I just didn't want to be one of those kids who needs parents. I've never really needed anyone before.

I dialed Gil's number. I was expecting his usual stammering voice. Instead, I heard an electronic voice that didn't stammer at all.

"The number you have reached is out of service. Please check the number and dial again." The voice was cold and lifeless. That's how I felt inside too. I started considering possibilities, and none of them were good. The best one I could think of was that the earthquakes had screwed up some cell towers. But now that I knew what, or more importantly, *who* was causing all the tremors, even that idea wasn't comforting. Without thinking, I started muttering the names of the Apollo astronauts in order of their missions.

"Virgil 'Gus' Grissom . . . Edward H. White . . . Roger Chaffee . . . Walter M. Schirra Jr. . . . ."

All of a sudden, Elena was shaking me.

"What's wrong, Logan? You're freaking me out!"

I tried to explain, but I realized that she was reacting to what I was telling her as if normal parents were out on a normal night not answering their normal cell phone. She didn't know that my foster parents were superheroes tracking down an earthquake-spewing bad guy. So I asked her to come outside with me. Then, as a Virgin American Airbus A320-200 went overhead, I told her the facts. I started with the weirdness of Gil never eating because he's actually a big ball of dark-matter-infused energy in a person suit. Then I moved on to the way Margie's skin reacts when it gets hot or hit by something heavy. I told her about MASC and the headquarters that used to be under the studio and the public pool paradox. I told her about Seismyxer and his different wristbands and headband, and the way he wasn't affected by Margie's telepathy.

I knew I wasn't supposed to tell her any of it, but my mind had come up with only two possibilities:

1. I could keep it to myself, head back to ESTO, and wait to see who came looking for me first.

2. I could tell the truth to the one person I really trusted and hope she would help me.

"That's the wildest thing I've ever heard . . . but I believe you, Logan."

I was shocked. Elena didn't even ask for proof. She

acted like my word was enough, and I'll admit . . . it felt kinda good.

"So the question is, what do we do now?"

I didn't really have an adequate reply ready, but once I regathered my thoughts, I realized that there might be clues in the house.

We went inside to look for Gil's laptop again, figuring any research they'd done might still be on it. We went through the house room by room, but the computer wasn't anywhere to be found.

"Maybe we should put on the news, Logan," Elena suggested. "It sounds like whenever this Seismyxer guy gets into a tight spot, big earthquakes follow. If he threw down with Gil and Margie, it probably registered on the Richter scale."

It was a good idea, so I showed Elena where the remote was and then went to the back of the house to check the one place I hadn't looked yet.

The keypad to the garage was at the end of the hall. Even though Gil had made sure I never saw what the code was, I knew what it sounded like.

That's something else I should tell you. The same thing that allows me to remember every word that's said to me also lets me remember musical notes too. Don't get me wrong. I'm an awful singer and I can't play any instruments. But I could remember the sequence of tones from the day I moved in; it was 31415926535. Those are also the first eleven digits of pi. Gil really is a nerd. Much respect.

Anyway, once I was in the garage, it looked just like how it did when I'd seen it last. That is a fact. It didn't look "kinda" like it did . . . it looked exactly how it did when Gil had given me a brief tour. None of the supplies had been moved an inch. It reminded me of Gil's dusty side of the closet, which meant nothing in the garage was what it seemed. All the rolls of wire and the racks of equipment had to be for show. So I searched around, lifting tools and turning knobs. Nothing. Then I saw it. Gil's lunch box was sitting on a shelf by the door. The thing is, Gil doesn't eat.

I walked over, flicked open the latch on the lunch box, and the entire garage transformed. Spools flipped over to reveal computer consoles. Lab equipment folded down from the racks of gear. And from under Gil's van, a bed slid out.

Now when I say *bed*, I'm not talking about a queen-size mattress and headboard. It was a glass tube with a platform inside and electromagnets positioned every few inches around the outside. And it had a pillow. I figured that was where Gil actually slept, if you can call it that. The magnets must have kept his dark-matter-infused molecules together. Either that or it was the world's coolest, biggest, most tricked-out, hyperbaric oxygen bed.

But the item I was most interested in was sitting on a

desk that slid out of the wall—Gil's laptop. It was open and plugged in. Luckily, Gil hadn't signed out before he'd left that morning. I guess he assumed his laptop would be safe in his supersecret garage headquarters. The browser was opened to the Caltech seismology lab website. I assumed Gil was using their earthquake maps to try and locate Seismyxer. I could see the logic, but without knowing what kind of patterns Gil and Margie had been looking for, I couldn't follow their thinking. I looked in the browser history and saw that he'd been surfing all over the Caltech site, including looking at the staff pages and the facilities. None of it made much sense.

"Logan, you should come in here! Quick!"

That was Elena, calling from the living room, so I tucked the computer under my arm and ran down the hall, where I found her watching the channel eight news. Terrell McKay was reporting from the scene of the studio implosion.

"Observers claim that there were multiple strong tremors before the Monolith Studios lot fell into the earth. Arthur Kang, owner of the local convenience store, Starwalk Mart, shot the shocking video we just showed you. Here it is again in slow motion."

Elena grabbed my shoulder and pointed at the screen. For a moment, I almost forgot to look at the screen because, well, she was touching my shoulder.

159

"This is what I wanted you to see."

At that point, the crisp HD picture on the television turned grainy and pixelated. It was reminiscent of Monet's various paintings of Rouen Cathedral from 1894, in that it wasn't as clear as a photo, but from far away, the pixels were enough to capture the real way it felt when the studio crumbled below street level. And then, amid all the dust and noise and Arthur Kang's finger blocking the lens a few times, you could see something shoot out of the rubble. It looked like it could have been a person . . . or two people . . . on a hoverboard, rising from the dust and zooming away into the rising sun.

After a beat, Terrell McKay was back on the screen.

"As you saw, it appeared that someone or something escaped the imploding studio and flew away on a device that resembles a flying surfboard. What was that device? Who was aboard it? And how are they connected to the most recent series of deadly earthquakes? The questions mount, as buildings continue to come crashing down. From a shaken Hollywood Boulevard, I'm Terrell McKay for channel eight news."

When the TV went back to the anchorwoman talking, Elena hit the mute button.

"That was the guy, wasn't it? Seismyxer? And it looked to me like he had someone with him."

I nodded. More importantly, the video had one detail

I hadn't been able to see in person. In slow motion, just before the sun's rays made the screen go white, I could see something about the person on the hoverboard with Seismyxer. He was wearing burgundy camouflage.

Then I got another idea. I opened up Gil's laptop and searched Google Maps for the location of Monolith Studios . . . and Caltech. Suddenly, it all made sense.

"Elena, do you think your dad would give me a ride somewhere without asking why I needed to go there?"

Elena looked at me and then shook her head with a smile that I couldn't quite figure out.

"No . . . so let's not ask him. I have a better idea."

11:28 P.M.
THURSDAY, OCTOBER 7

Here's two more things you should know about me: first, I'm not good at catching things, and second, I don't like to break the law.

On page 12 of the State of California's online *Driver Handbook*, it says people between the ages of 15 ½ and 17 ½ can obtain a learner's permit. However, on the next page, it makes it clear that individuals with a permit may only drive a motor vehicle when accompanied by a licensed driver over the age of 25.

And yet there I was, the only passenger in a cream-colored, 1988 BMW 318, as Elena (who isn't even old enough to have her permit yet) drove us toward Pasadena. One of the downsides of having an eidetic memory and having read just about everything is that if I break a law, it's not like I can claim I didn't know I was doing it.

But driving with Elena wasn't the first law I had broken that night.

Two hours earlier, Elena had gone back into her father's house and told him she was going to sleep at her mother's. She then had me stand next to her mother's house, in the dark, and wait by a window. This felt odd and wrong, but Elena assured me it would be okay, so I did it. Moments later, I watched as Elena walked in and told her mom that she'd be sleeping at her father's house for the night. And then, when her mother gave her a hug good night, Elena reached around her mother's back and grabbed her car keys off the counter. In one motion, she whipped them out the open window over to me.

I tracked them with my eyes and concentrated on raising my hands to catch the keys, but they hit me in the neck instead and made me gag a little.

Then we waited for both of her parents to fall asleep so we could steal her mom's car. At which point, I became an accessory to my first crime: grand theft auto.

"So where are we headed, Logan?" Elena asked, never taking her eyes off the road. Her father started teaching her to drive when she was thirteen. She was a confident but careful driver. In fact, she was one of the few people on the road who wasn't eating, arguing, or looking at their phone for directions.

I thought it was really cool that Elena was willing to help me find Gil and Margie without even knowing where we were going. It was like she trusted me, which was a new experience.

"When Seismyxer left MASC, he flew right into the rising sun. That means he flew east, because that's the direction the sun rises."

Elena shot me a look. "I know I don't have a super-brain, Logan, but give me a little credit."

For a second, I thought she was actually mad. Then she grinned, so I figured it was okay.

"Right . . . sorry . . . so what's east of Hollywood? I mean, other than most of the rest of the United States?"

"Pasadena," Elena responded, "but I'm only saying that because you told me we needed to drive toward Pasadena."

"Good listening. Yes. That is a fact. And what is also a fact is that Caltech is in Pasadena. The note Gil and Margie left said that Dr. Chrysler had given them a lead about where to find Seismyxer. Not *how* to find Seismyxer but *where*. That's why they were looking on the website for the Caltech Seismological Lab. They weren't tracking the earthquakes. They thought that's where Seismyxer took Colonel Gdula, so that's where they went."

"Why do you think Seismyxer took that colonel dude?"

I'd been thinking about that question and had narrowed things down to two possibilities:

1. Seismyxer didn't get what he was looking for when he attacked MASC, so he took the person with the most information. That also means he's got one of the only people who knows how to find Gil and Margie and me.

2. The whole reason Seismyxer attacked when and how he did was because he had someone on the inside working with him. And that was the person he took with him after destroying the base.

I relayed both these possibilities to Elena, and we agreed neither of them was very good. Then we both got really quiet as we pulled into the parking lot of the Caltech Seismological Lab, which was closed for the night.

Elena found a spot in the corner, away from any street-lights, where we had a good view of anyone coming or going from the lab.

"The most logical approach," I explained, "is to track off-hours traffic in or out of the building. If we notice any patterns or evidence of Seismyxer, we can use what we've observed to formulate a plan for getting inside."

"Logan, you can just say, 'We gotta keep an eye on the lab.'"

She had a point. So that's what we did, sitting in silence, waiting for anything to happen as my mind wandered a little. I leaned my head against the window to think about everything that had happened in the past twenty-four hours. The movie theater . . . the studio-tour-turned-headquarters tour . . . the bus rides . . . all those bus rides . . .

The next thing I knew, Elena was tapping me on the shoulder and the sun was blaring right into my eyes between two buildings.

"What happened? Where are we? Why is the sun up?"

That was me. Elena looked over from the driver's seat of the car with a funny kind of smile.

"Okay, in order: you fell asleep because you'd been up for thirty-six hours straight, so I stayed up all night keeping watch, even though *nothing* happened. We're still parked in the Caltech lot. And the sun is up because this part of Earth is now facing it." She paused. "You know, it's fun being the one with the answers for once."

I sat up in the passenger seat and quickly wiped the drool off the corner of my mouth as I looked at the clock in the car. It was 8:48 a.m. I'd been out for over eight hours, but I definitely needed it.

"So now what, Sleeping Beauty?"

It was a fair question. Across the parking lot, the Seismological Lab building was just a short walk away and I knew it was time to get out of the car and try to save the day. But I also knew I had no idea what I was about to get us into.

I'd run through all the possible outcomes in my

head—about 47 percent of them involved Gil and/or Margie being dead. Of course, I'd also thought about what might happen to me if Gil and Margie were alive and Seismyxer barged in on me trying to rescue them—about 100 percent of those scenarios resulted in me winding up dead too.

"Here's what I'm thinking," I said, trying to sound confident. "I'll go in and look around while you go tell someone what's going on."

I don't know if I said that to be brave, or because I was feeling guilty that I was risking her life to save my foster parents. But before I could say more, Elena was already shaking her head.

"Who would I tell, Logan? The police? The press? Campus security? No one would believe me. Besides, even if they could help us, it would still be the end for Gil and Margie."

I was confused at that point, so I told Elena, "I'm confused. If we saved Gil and Margie, why would it be the end of them?"

"Because we'd only be saving their superhero lives, Logan. Not their secret identity lives. Everyone would know. For Gil and Margie—and anyone else whose secret identities suddenly weren't secret—they couldn't just be anonymous anymore. Being a normal person would be gone forever . . . and that's the really important part, Logan.

That's what the comic books get wrong. From what you said, Gil and Margie just want to be a married couple and parents—your parents—and to live their lives. Frankly, I bet most heroes do too. Maybe some of them will keep being heroes even after it's all in the open. I bet more than a few will. But the chance for them to ever feel normal, even for a little while, that's gone forever."

I wasn't sure I agreed with *everything* Elena said; but listening to her, I realized that even though I'd been running possibilities through my mind, I'd never looked at the situation from Gil and Margie's point of view.

"You're right." I nodded to Elena. "But that still doesn't mean you have to come in with me. You could—"

I was about to list other possibilities for how Elena could help, when she got out of the car and started walking toward the building. I rushed to catch up.

"I wouldn't have come this far if I wasn't planning to help you all the way. We're in this together, so you can miss me with the noise about me staying outside. That isn't happening. It's sexist and it's cliché and it's a bad idea. No offense."

I didn't take any offense. She was right. I've seen 312 action movies in my life where someone has told someone else to "stay outside" to keep them safe. It never works.

As I nodded, it dawned on me that Elena didn't seem at all freaked out by everything she'd seen and learned in the past day.

So I said, "You don't seem at all freaked out by everything. I'm not sure that's a very typical reaction."

Elena crossed her arms and turned to me. "I've never been all that typical, Logan. I'm biracial, bilingual, taller than everyone in my class, faster, and I . . . well, I'm the only person I know who lives in two houses on the same street. I guess I've just grown up expecting the weird stuff to happen because it always has. Worrying about what's 'normal' . . . it's just a waste of time."

And I understood what she was saying, so I nodded . . . but I was also kind of amazed. Every day that I can remember—and I can remember just about all of them since that day in the airport—I've woken up wondering whether there is such a thing as *normal* and if so, what it feels like. Maybe that's why I want to find you so badly: normal kids have families.

I didn't say any of that to Elena. I just kept nodding.

"We make a good pair of misfits, you and I." Elena took my hand and led me toward the lab. Realizing we were holding hands, I involuntarily began reciting the manifest of the RMS *Lusitania*. It was sunk by a U-boat on May 7, 1915.

At this point, it was almost 9 a.m. Other than grad students and scientists, there weren't many people around.

"So how are we going to get in there, Logan?"

Sometimes, when people ask me a question, I have to scan through thousands or even millions of pieces of information. But at that moment, I didn't need to do anything but keep my eyes open. Just beyond Elena's shoulder, I saw trio of yellow school buses pulling into the parking lot.

"We're going to blend in with one of these field trips. When the kids get off those buses, we just step in line and head inside with them."

And that's exactly what we did.

Actually, it wasn't *exactly* what we did. The first field trip was from an all-girls' school. Needless to say, I don't think I would have been able to fit in.

So we waited outside for the next bunch of buses to arrive. The whole time, I was holding Margie's cell phone, thinking about the special number she'd given me that would call in the MASC commandos. It was twenty-three digits long and included pound signs. As I ran through all the possibilities of what was about to happen and how many of them ended badly for me and Elena, I really considered dialing it. But before I could decide which was more unwise—calling MASC or going in with zero backup—two more buses from a public school arrived and we joined the students without anyone noticing.

Inside, we stayed with the tour for the first ten minutes as a grad student led us around the building.

"We are currently experiencing more seismic events per day than we've seen in recorded history," the grad student announced as she led us down the hall. Most of the students seemed to be more interested in updating their Snapchat stories than listening. Several of them had their phones taken away by their teacher.

But the most interesting part of the tour came when we came to a stairwell and I was able to look at the floor diagram on the evacuation placard.

"Checking it out in case we have to get away fast?"

That was Elena, talking in a whisper even though no one was close by.

"This should show every room, every stairway, and every door on the ground floor. If Seismyxer has a secret entrance . . . I'm betting that door isn't listed on the evacuation plan. So all we have to do is find a door that isn't on this map. But knowing the fastest way out is a good idea too."

Elena shook her head and smiled. "You could be dangerous if you ever used that brain for evil. Let's go."

We ditched the tour as the class went upstairs, and we made our way back down the hall we'd just come in through. I compared every doorway we passed to what I'd seen on the evacuation diagram. I quickly realized that the map I'd seen wasn't really drawn to scale. That is a fact, and it's a shame. An institution of science like Caltech should really pay more attention to the details.

Anyway, I had assumed it would be pretty easy to find

the entrance to Seismyxer's hideout, but after one loop around the entire first floor, I hadn't spotted anything suspicious.

"We must have missed something. I'm sure of it."

And I *was* sure of it, so we took another lap. This time I was studying access panels in the walls and floor, looking for signs that they'd been moved recently. I was so focused that I didn't even notice Elena hissing at me.

"Logan . . . stop!" she said, and before I could figure out why, I was flat on the floor and my skin was burning and wet. For a second. I wondered if I'd been attacked by a supervillain with acid breath or lava snot or something. I braced myself for another attack.

"Logan? What are you . . . ?"

That was Dr. Chrysler. He was wearing a Caltech lab coat drenched in fresh coffee and was standing over me with a puzzled look. I couldn't blame him. I was pretty puzzled too.

Dr. Chrysler's mouth hung open as Elena helped me up off the floor. I couldn't tell at first if he was stammering because he was surprised to see us or because he was just really upset about his coffee.

"What are you doing here?"

"We're looking for Gil and Margie," I explained. "That's why you're here too, right? Are you undercover? Did MASC make you that fake ID? Was that hazelnut coffee? I'm allergic to hazelnuts."

Dr. Chrysler didn't answer my questions right away, and I noticed his eyes going back and forth from me to Elena, who was now standing just behind me with her arms crossed.

"It's okay. She knows about my foster parents . . . and about MASC . . . and about everything else. I had to tell her. She's my friend . . . and my ride." Dr. Chrysler looked like he was about to say something, so I kept talking. "I am aware that it's probably an international security breach, but a supervillain just destroyed your West Coast HQ, so I'm guessing that a high school volleyball player knowing a few secrets isn't your top concern."

"Hey! I'm not just a high school volleyball player!" Elena interrupted. "I also run track, play basketball, *and* I'm the class treasurer."

"But how did you end up here? Did your foster parents tell you to come?"

Dr. Chrysler was whispering, and I realized then that I'd been talking pretty loud about stuff that I probably should have been whispering about too.

I quietly explained how I figured out where to go.

"That's all you needed? A browser history and the evening news? That's . . . impressive."

"Technically, you gave Gil and Margie the tip first. So how did *you* figure out this is where Seismyxer has been hiding out?" I asked. "Did you know that he took Colonel Gdula? Do you think Gdula might be a mole? Do you think—"

Dr. Chrysler held up his finger to his lips. It's a well-known signal to be quiet. That is a fact.

"We shouldn't have this conversation here. Why don't you and . . . um . . ."

"Elena." She spoke up, which was good because I had forgotten to introduce her.

"Of course . . . Elena. Why don't you come with me? I know a better place for us to talk. Follow me and don't speak until we're there. Okay? Can you do that, Logan?"

I told him I could, so Dr. Chrysler led us down the hall, nodding every so often at passing grad students and scientists like he knew them. I thought that was odd for someone who was working undercover. However, I had promised not to say anything, so I just added it to the end of the long list of questions I was going to ask once we could talk again.

After a few turns, Dr. Chrysler led us to a door that read "Emerging Technologies Lab—Authorized Personnel Only," and he swiped a key card that opened the security door.

The lab had no windows at all. The walls were gleaming white and the perimeter of the room was populated with high-tech machines. The only breaks in the technology were the door we'd come in through and a small gap between two banks of servers on the far wall. As I was looking around, Dr. Chrysler picked up a phone on a desk and dialed an extension.

"We have special guests in the lab," he quickly

explained to whomever was on the other end of the line. "Can you join us? Excellent." He hung up and smiled at us. "This is much better. We're away from prying eyes. I can finally let you know exactly what is going on."

I told Dr. Chrysler that I appreciated it because I was very confused. I added that it is a condition I do not enjoy.

"We will clear that up at once, Logan," Dr. Chrysler explained, as I heard a door open behind us, which was strange, because there wasn't any door behind us when we came in. "But first, I want to make a formal introduction. Of course, I believe you two have met before."

I turned and saw a much bigger man had entered the lab. He had on a lab coat just like Dr. Chrysler's, but unlike Dr. Chrysler, he did not look at all like a scientist. In fact, he looked like Seismyxer, and he was holding something in his hand. Suddenly, that "something" flashed.

And then, everything went dark.

1:12 P.M.
FRIDAY, OCTOBER 8

Are you a morning person? That's the term people use when someone is good at waking up. I find it an odd way to divide up the population. Everyone you see during the day eventually succeeded at waking up. If they didn't, they'd still be in bed. That said . . . I am a morning person. As soon as my eyes open, my brain starts going and I'm usually ready to do things.

I said "usually" because this time was different. This time, when I opened my eyes, I wasn't even sure I was alive.

I felt like I was floating. The first thing I saw was a brilliant, bright light, and the world smelled of citrus verbena.

I thought I might be in heaven (which I have yet to find proof that it exists), but after a second, I realized that the brightness was just bad fluorescent lighting. I felt like I was floating because I was on a cart going down a hallway. And the citrus scent was Elena's shampoo. Her hair was in my face. Someone had bound our wrists and then tethered us together, back-to-back, with high-tech bungee cords.

The cart stopped and two burly security guys dressed in all black released the bungees that held us together. Then they hoisted Elena and me up to our feet. We weren't in the lab anymore. At least not the lab as it looked a moment ago. It seemed like they'd taken us to a sort of underground installation, with heavy metal blast doors between rooms and ceilings that were carved out of rough stone. In front of us stood Dr. Chrysler and Seismyxer, one of whom was no longer in a lab coat.

"Welcome, Logan. What do you think of our little facility?"

With its long halls and surveillance cameras . . . it actually looked a lot like MASC HQ.

"It looks a lot like MASC HQ."

"I did help design both of them. This one has many of the same amenities, with a few upgrades and far fewer celebrities wandering around on the surface. Come along."

By this point, I had figured out that most of what I knew about Dr. Chrysler was a lie. But the two things

I knew were 100 percent true were as follows: the guy liked building underground installations . . . and giving tours of them.

There were labs, control rooms, and even a room full of computers with two Houdini chairs. But then we were escorted into the Containment Unit. That's what he called it, and I guess it was a pretty appropriate name. Inside were five customized cells; and as I was walked past them, I saw they each had a superhero inside, trapped and looking in rough shape.

The first one held TideStrider, who I had met just a day before at MASC. They had him in an arid, plexiglass box with a giant heat lamp blaring down on him. His skin and lips looked parched and cracked.

I squinted at the next hero, but I didn't recognize him at all. He was a big guy with arms that looked like they were made of rock. His body was hunched over, and his hands were locked into a solid block of metal that was welded to the floor. I couldn't help wondering if this was Quarry Lord, one of the heroes Colonel Gdula had said was missing.

In the third cell, there was a heroine who I was sure had to be FemmeFlorance. Her entire body was made up of symbiotic plant cells. She was dressed just like in the comic books, and I remembered Gdula saying she'd gone missing too. Her prison appeared to be a glorified meat locker, with cold air pumping in to cover her in frost. She looked like a spring crocus that had bloomed too early. But as I looked closer, I realized I didn't just recognize her from the comics. I had met her.

It was Genevieve, the very nice Frenchwoman from the Botanical Gardens. She looked different than she did in her gardener's uniform, but her brilliant green eyes gave her away. Suddenly, I understood why Gil and Margie had lied that day. They weren't ashamed of me. They were worried she'd report what she saw to MASC.

I was still thinking about it when I was snapped back into the moment by Elena shouting. "Gil! Margie!"

Elena pointed at the final two cells, and it took me a moment to understand exactly what I was looking at. Gil and Margie were each in their own cell, and both looked like they were suffering.

"What are you doing to them?"

"Containing them in the most effective way I know how, Logan. Margie's cell is fitted with a specially calibrated electromagnet that exerts a force seventy-two times that of Earth's gravity on the alien metal in her skin. Oh, and the glass has been coated in a telepathy-canceling isotope so she can't 'talk' her way out."

She was on her knees, clearly in pain from the pressure of the magnetic force.

Gil looked even worse. Within his cell, his hands, feet, and the top of his head were all cinched into metallic spheres. Every few seconds, seemingly at random, one of the five balls would discharge a burst of light, and the part of Gil's body that was nearest to that sphere would disappear and then re-form. Each time after it happened, Gil howled in agony.

"Dark matter collectors on his extremities, pulling at his molecules, interrupted by randomized neutrino bursts," Dr. Chrysler explained in a way that made me think he was proud of it.

I asked the most obvious question. I've found that it's usually the one that is most important, and yet people never seem to ask it. "Why are you doing this?"

"Why am I doing this?" He gestured at the heroes he had contained in the room. "You mean betraying MASC? Good question."

But he didn't answer. Instead his security guards shoved us toward the door. On the way out, I looked back and saw Margie raise her head up, just an inch or two. Our eyes met, and I saw one of her quicksilver tears well up. But then the magnet got ahold of it, and instead of rolling down her cheek, it slammed into the floor at the speed of sound and made a ping loud enough to ring out through the room.

The blast doors closed behind us then, and Dr. Chrysler started monologuing again.

"For decades, I worked for MASC, advancing the cause, never asking what was in it for me. I found ways to distill certain heroes' powers and to amplify the abilities of others. All the while, I grew older and older. Never richer nor happier, mind you. Just older."

Elena laughed, but not in a way like she thought it was funny. "You sold out everyone you know for money? That's so weak."

If Dr. Chrysler took offense, he didn't show it. "Oh, the pay is definitely better on this side, but this isn't about money. It's about power, and who has it. MASC grew more powerful, despite having almost no real power other than the ability to coerce superhumans into joining the cause. Anyone who disobeyed or dared to make decisions for themselves was declared a villain and then MASC would send their heroes to root out these so-called enemies. The hypocrisy was undeniable.

"Then I was approached by Necros. I assumed she wished to abduct me or even destroy me. Instead, she helped me understand that, eventually, all these powerful individuals would realize that they didn't have to follow orders. When that happens, there will be a war between the humans, who need to feel like they're at the top of the evolutionary ladder, and the superhumans, who actually are at the apex. And I chose which side I'll be on when that war comes."

We moved down the halls and I was careful to make sure I was memorizing the layout. Turns out there aren't many clear exit signs in an evil lair.

"There were other factors, of course," Dr. Chrysler continued. "With Necros, I'm free to study the powers *I* find most fascinating. All Gdula and the rest of his camo-wearing cronies cared about was building a tactical advantage. If a power couldn't be used in a fight, it was totally ignored. For example, did you know the Flash could get a full night's sleep in thirty seconds? Of course you didn't. MASC thought it was a big yawn, pun intended.

"But maybe the most compelling reason for my switch has been the access I've received to one of the most unique superhumans on the planet. Necros's ability to drain an organism's life force and convert it into energy that sustains and heals her . . . that could be a fountain of youth. I'm not saying I wish to live forever . . . but I couldn't turn down the chance to give it a try."

At that point, we were escorted through a pair of heavy doors and into what must have been their version of a jail for regular humans. It was far less impressive than the Containment Unit. The hallway split a pair of long cells, each with a set of bunk beds, a toilet, and fifteen-foot-tall bars that went up nearly to the ceiling. Elena and I were both freed from the bonds on our wrists, and then she was escorted into the cell on the right. I was deposited in the one across the hall.

"You know, Logan, when you first showed up, I was

worried that you were going to be a complication. But your presence may actually make it easier to talk sense to your foster parents. They are quite fond of you, as am I. Studying your mind might be every bit as illuminating as the work I've done on any superhero. In fact, I think your entire foster family could be a welcome addition to our efforts. Think about it."

With that, he turned and left with the guards. Only when they were gone did I really look around, and that's when I realized I had a cellmate. He was a maroon-camo-clad man, sitting in the shadows on the bottom bunk at the back of the cell . . . and he was the last person I wanted to see at the moment.

"I assume you've figured out that Gil and Margie weren't the moles, Colonel," I said, matter-of-factly, because it was a fact.

"Logan, who is that? Who are you talking to?"

That was Elena, calling over from her cell while her hands nervously tested the strength of the bars.

"It's Colonel Gdula," I replied. "I told you about him. He's the one who's always angry and rarely right about things."

"I can admit when I'm wrong," Gdula grumbled. "After seeing that piece of dirt, Chrysler, walking around here like a turkey the day after Thanksgiving, I realized what really happened. But you aren't totally off the hook, boy! If you and your *foster parents* hadn't been in our HQ in the first place, distracting my security team, none of us would be in this mess."

"Hey! Don't blame Logan for your weak-sauce security," Elena shouted out from her cell. I appreciated that she was on my side.

"And besides," I said pointedly to Gdula, "Seismyxer didn't attack to get Gil or Margie, or me for that matter. He left with only one person under his arm, which means he was there for you."

"Think you're pretty smart, don't you, kid? I was the consolation prize. Necros and the doc sent Seismyxer to intercept our database download."

I had to admit that that made a lot more sense.

"That makes a lot more sense."

"The information in that database is all they need to either recruit, blackmail, or ambush every superhuman on the planet," Colonel Gdula grumbled, visibly fuming. "Chrysler set the whole thing up. They might've gotten what they wanted if that fracas in the control room hadn't destroyed the mainframe. But when the computer got wrecked, Seismyxer blew a gasket and grabbed me, figuring I must know something that could help them."

"Do you?"

"Apparently not enough." Gdula stood up from the bottom bunk. Once the light hit his face, I could see that one of his eyes was swollen shut and his bottom lip was split. "When they realize I don't have any backdoor, top secret access, they'll either try to ransom me back to MASC, which won't work, or they'll kill me . . . which probably will work."

"Kill you? Why? I mean, they've got you locked up," Elena asked from across the hall. Colonel Gdula snorted.

"Dunno how you got mixed up in this, little lady, but if I've learned anything in four decades as a soldier, it is that the only enemy you don't need to worry about . . . is a dead one. They'll kill me, and if they can't turn Logan or his *foster folks* into assets, they'll do the same to you all." Colonel Gdula sat back down on the bunk bed and his face disappeared into the shadows again.

"It's what I'd do if I were them."

8:34 P.M.
FRIDAY, OCTOBER 8

I wouldn't be surprised if you're feeling kind of tense right now, reading about your big brother locked in a cell, surrounded by supervillains. I promise you; I was feeling just as tense living it.

For about seven hours, I ran through options for finding a way out. The cell I was in wasn't special, not compared to what was holding Gil and Margie. I considered every article and book I'd ever read on escaping captivity, including all 544 pages in the paperback edition of *The Last Escape: The Untold Story of Allied Prisoners of War in Europe 1944–45* by John Nichol and Tony Rennel.

The whole time, Colonel Gdula was absolutely no help.

Every time I shared an idea with Elena across the hall, he'd tell me why it wouldn't work—or, worse, just laugh.

To be fair, it wasn't like Elena was coming up with any ideas either. She spent several hours not doing much more than sitting in a chair, looking up at the ceiling.

"Are you thinking we might be able to tunnel up to get out?" I asked.

"No, I was just . . . I mean . . . I dunno."

Elena got quiet again and went back to looking at the ceiling.

A few hours later, some guards showed up, pressed the button at the end of the hall to unlock the doors, and gave us dinner. We'd just finished when Dr. Chrysler came back, flanked by a pair of beefy security guys who looked like they just stepped out of a video game. Each one was toting a big, futuristic gun as well.

"Would you please come with us, Logan?"

"Do I have a choice?" I replied. "The guys with the guns make me think it's not really a request."

Two seconds later, I was lifted up by the back of my shirt and removed from the cell.

Elena yelled at the guards, "Where are you taking him? Hey! I'm talking to you!"

But Dr. Chrysler and his goons weren't in a chatty mood. They took me back to the Containment Unit, where Seismyxer was waiting, standing next to a very small, inarguably beautiful woman. Her hair was dark and her skin was pale, at least what I could see of it. She wore a long gown that touched the ground and dragged a good three feet behind her.

She looked like she could be a movie star, but I knew before we were even introduced that she wasn't.

"Come, my child."

She was Necros. She spoke in a voice lower and huskier than I'd expected. When she held out her hand, I noticed that she wore long, black velvet gloves that ran up past her elbows. I remembered what Dr. Chrysler had said about her powers—the ability to steal life through a simple touch. It's a serious superpower, and I didn't want to find out whether it worked through velvet. I stepped toward her very, very carefully.

"What's the matter, kid? Afraid to shake a lady's hand?" Seismyxer laughed.

Necros glared at Seismyxer and he stopped smiling, but that didn't make me feel any better.

Dr. Chrysler walked up alongside me. "I assure you, Logan, you're safe . . . at least for the moment."

"Why should I believe you?"

"As someone who has spent much of my life surrounded by enemies and threats, I know what you're feeling." Necros sighed. "But the truth is that you are very valuable to us, because you are apparently very valuable to them."

With that, Necros held up a small remote control in the direction of Gil's and Margie's cells, and pressed a button. Almost immediately, I could see that she had dialed down the power on their restraints. The charges that scrambled Gil's molecules went from huge shocks to a low hum. It still made him look like a pixelated TV screen every few seconds, but it seemed less painful now. And Margie was able to slowly pull herself off the magnetic floor.

"Quicksilver Siren . . . Ultra-Quantum . . . I brought Logan here to make you an offer. Join us in our battle to end superhuman slavery and servitude. Claim your rightful places above the petty regulation of humans. Help us dismantle the abomination that is MASC, so people like us can live out in the open, without hiding our powers, and finally decide for ourselves how we wish to use our gifts."

"You think you're a saint," Margie spat out, finally rising all the way to her feet. "But you're just a killer. And now you're threatening to kill an innocent boy. Why would we ever want to ally ourselves with someone like you?"

Necros paused and furrowed her eyebrows, though it wasn't too much of a furrow since her eyebrows are really well-groomed and thin.

"In any revolution, there are innocents hurt before justice prevails. But I have not suggested I was going to harm Logan. My intention is quite the opposite. Pledge yourselves to our cause, and in exchange, I will offer you what

MASC never would. I will help you keep your family together."

"What do you mean?" Gil asked, in between the bursts of being atomized.

"Do you think MASC will allow you to keep him? They'll lie and claim it isn't safe for superhumans to have children. They won't let you raise Logan because MASC exists to control you. However, if you swear allegiance to freeing our kind, you can have a family. You can live your life. You will have the same rights as every other person."

In terms of a bargaining tactic, Necros's offer was impressive and totally unexpected. I watched as my foster parents looked at each other wordlessly. Then Margie turned back to Necros.

"I don't believe you. You'll say anything to get what you want, and Logan will never be safe. Not with you . . . and not with us. If you want us to trust you . . . you have to prove you won't hurt him."

"And how would I do that?"

I was wondering the same thing.

"Make him safe. Erase us from his memories and take him back to the orphanage."

9:09 P.M.
FRIDAY, OCTOBER 8

I may not know what every emotional reaction looks like. But there was no mistaking the surprised looks in the room when Margie asked for me to have my memory wiped. Gil's jaw dropped open until he was zapped by another pulse of magnetic energy. Seismyxer even went as far as to mouth the word *huh?* But there was one person who didn't react that way. Necros.

"How fascinating . . ." she said.

"But only two days ago, you were willing to tear MASC apart to keep them from touching Logan's memories and taking him away from you," Dr. Chrysler argued. "I must say, if this is a scheme, it's an utterly mind-boggling one."

Margie glared at Dr. Chrysler like she wanted to do more than boggle his mind.

"Two days ago, I thought that having us as his parents was the best thing for Logan. I believed we could keep him safe. But now . . . this is what any *real* mother would do." Margie turned to look at me and I saw the silver tears welling up in her eyes, once again only to be pulled to the floor by the magnets below.

"Logan, I'm sorry we got you into all this. As awful as it sounds . . . wiping your memories and sending you back to ESTO is the best thing for you."

I looked at Gil to see if he agreed. He's generally less emotional than Margie, which I appreciate.

"She's right, Logan." He sighed. "If you think about it logically . . . it's the only way."

And then it got quiet again.

"How do we know," Necros said, breaking the silence, "that once Logan is safely away, you won't turn on us? At that point, what have you got to lose?"

It was a good question.

"Actually, we're the only ones with something to lose at that point." It was Gil who spoke. "Logan won't . . . well, he won't remember us, but we'll remember him. And we know that if we break the deal, you'll . . . you know where to find him. It's something we'd never risk."

It was like they were playing chess with each other, and I was the pawn. I can't say I liked it much.

"I don't like this," I told them. "Don't I get a say in what's best for me?"

All five of the adults in the room said no at the same time.

"So this is our bargain?" Necros asked formally, like the words were a contract. Of course, words can be a contract as evidenced by court cases, including 1962's *Joachim v. Weldon*, 2010's *K. Miller Construction Company, Inc. v. Joseph J. McGinnis et al.*, and literally hundreds of others. "You pledge to join us in exchange for Logan's total ignorance and safety?"

Gil and Margie looked at each other wordlessly, and this time, they both nodded.

"And Elena too," Margie added. "His friend. You have to send her back too with no memory of any of this . . . or him."

"Then it is sealed." Necros bowed her head formally and walked with Dr. Chrysler out the door. Once they left, Seismyxer shook his head and laughed through clenched teeth.

"You two are the worst negotiators ever. When I joined up, I got promised Indonesia. The whole country. Surf, sun, and all the seismic activity I could ever want. You guys just chucked it all for a twerp who isn't going to even remember you."

It looked like Margie and Gil were about to say something to me, but before they could, Seismyxer turned up the dials so high on both of their cells that neither of them could speak.

As Seismyxer walked me down the hall, we met up with Elena, flanked by two of the guards, and all of us began walking together toward the room with the Houdini chairs.

"What's happening, Logan?"

That was Elena, whispering to me, though I'm sure the guards could hear us.

"They're going to wipe our memories and send us back to our old lives."

"That doesn't make any sense," Elena insisted. "Are they sending Gil and Margie back too?"

I told her she was the only one going back to Kittyhawk Circle and explained the rest of the deal.

"Logan, this is crazy." She whispered even quieter, "As soon as we're safe, I'll come find you. We'll figure this out. Okay?"

I had to explain to her that she wouldn't even remember meeting me and that I wouldn't remember meeting her or Gil and Margie either. And when I started thinking about that fact, that I wouldn't remember the only foster parents who had wanted to keep me plus the only cool friend I'd ever had . . . that's when I started getting really upset.

I started babbling: books and website URLs for my favorite cat videos and entire lists of data.

"Logan, what's happening to you? Talk to me!"

Elena was begging me to snap out of it, but I couldn't. By the time we were escorted into the room with the Houdini chairs, I had spouted out several pages of the Dungeons & Dragons *Monster Manual*, recited the appendix of a world atlas, and listed all the colors up to mauve in the song "Joseph's Coat" from the musical *Joseph and the Technicolor Dreamcoat*.

Seismyxer went to join Necros, off to the side, while Dr. Chrysler listened to another guy in a lab coat.

"We've never calibrated the chair to erase this much memory, Dr. Chrysler. Usually it's just a few hours. A day or two at most. You're suggesting purging almost a whole month of memories."

"It's a formula, Dr. Isenberg. We merely enter how many hours we wish to erase . . ."

That's when the other scientist, Dr. Isenberg, pulled out a tablet. "But as you see, within the formula, there is an exponential relationship between the length of the memory to be erased and the margin of error. The standard deviation we see when erasing one hour is almost nonexistent, but when you go to two hours, it doubles, though it's still a minuscule risk. At three, it doubles again, and so on. You're asking us to erase up to seven hundred hours of his memory."

"At very least," Dr. Chrysler agreed, nodding. "So

what are your concerns?"

The other scientist shrugged. I got the feeling he wasn't the type of scientist who shrugged all that often. "Permanent brain damage. Hemispheric interpolation. A loss of months, even years. We have no idea what this amount of exposure will do to a normal human mind."

"And we still won't," Dr. Chrysler assured him, giving me a look that I didn't appreciate. "Logan's mind is anything but normal. But let's document the results regardless."

"You can't do this to him! Not to his memory!" Elena lunged forward despite the restraints binding her hands. It took two guards to hold her back.

Two other security guards dragged me toward the Houdini chair as Dr. Chrysler pulled out a notebook. I knew there was no way he was going to change his mind, so I turned my attention to Necros.

"Please. You don't have to do this to me! I'm no threat to you."

This seemed to intrigue her because with a simple hand raise, her security goons put me down.

"If there's one thing I've learned in my centuries on this planet, it's that knowledge really is power, Logan. You have seen our installation. You know the truth about Dr. Chrysler—and about our plans. We can't let that stand. Your foster parents understand, which is why they offered their bargain."

I knew what she was saying was right. But I also knew that she didn't know me.

"You don't know me. No one listens to me. Never. I'm an orphan. I don't even know my real name. I am always the youngest kid in my grade and the smallest and the one with the fewest friends. That is a fact. It doesn't matter what I know or what I tell people. No one will care. No one ever cares."

Necros frowned a little. Not a mean frown, at least I don't think so. More like a soft frown.

"I do understand. I know what it is like to have abilities that could be an asset if others weren't so confused by them. In fact, that is exactly why I despise MASC and everything they stand for. A century ago, I learned of this new entity, MASC, and I offered my services to them. To the world, really. After several lifetimes of using my abilities to remain young and amass a fortune, I saw an opportunity to have my powers studied and used for the greater good. I was even willing to give up my powers if such a thing was possible. After all, I had never asked for them . . . and I was not always proud of how I had used them."

She stepped toward me as she removed her glove and regarded her hand. It looked like a normal hand to me. In fact, it looked like a kinda perfect hand to me. Not the kind of hand that had spent the last few hundred years draining the life out of innocent victims.

"Yet when I extended my hand in friendship, MASC

said my powers could never be anything but deadly and dark. Instead of inviting me in, they called me a monster and tried to capture me, so I fought back. I won't deny it. I had taken lives before that—some by accident, others by choice. But *they* made me a villain that day, and ever since, I've only wanted to watch the puppet masters come crashing down."

Necros was just about the most powerful person on the planet—but I found myself thinking, at least in that moment, that in a lot of ways she wasn't all the different from me. She didn't want to feel like there was anything wrong with her either.

"I don't want to bring anyone crashing down," I admitted. "I just want to have a family, some friends maybe, and to feel normal for once."

I looked over to Elena and saw that tears were rolling down her face. I couldn't tell if they were angry tears or sad ones. I wasn't sure if there was even a difference.

Necros put her glove back on and then she put her hand on my shoulder. I flinched, afraid she'd drain the life force from my body. Velvet is a pretty flimsy fabric after all. But she didn't. "Then don't think of this as us taking anything from you, my child. Think of it as us giving you something else: a chance to truly find the things you're looking for. Because these people aren't your real family. And as long as you're a part of any of this . . . *normal* will never be within your grasp."

And with that, she gestured toward the security guards, who strapped me into the Houdini chair. I didn't fight it. Elena was calling to me, but I tried not to listen because I knew I wouldn't remember any of it in a few seconds. Elena, Margie, Gil . . . I might not even remember that I was your big brother if things went wrong.

I started panicking. A steady stream of dates and names and addresses came cascading out of my mouth like liquid chocolate over the waterfall on page 63 of Roald Dahl's *Charlie and the Chocolate Factory*. I didn't even know what I was saying as they strapped me into the chair and put the headpiece on . . . but apparently, Dr. Chrysler did.

"Stop! Take it off. Now!"

Dr. Chrysler was waving his arms and pushing everyone away.

9:36 P.M.
FRIDAY, OCTOBER 8

Dr. Chrysler stopped the procedure before it could start wiping my memory. I wasn't sure what was going on.

"What were you saying just now? What *was* that?" he asked, leaning in way too close to me. He pried the head-piece off my scalp in a single yank, taking a few clumps of hair with it. It really hurt; those connectors are super sticky. Dr. Chrysler was waiting for an answer, his face just a few inches from mine. I clearly wasn't the only person who hadn't brushed his teeth in a few days.

"It's a list," I told him. "I recite lists of things when I'm panicking."

Necros's eyebrows rose, but she didn't speak.

"Continue the list, just as you were speaking it," Dr. Chrysler insisted. "This may be your only chance."

I glanced over at Elena, who was still being restrained. But she managed a small nod. "Go on!"

I started talking, even though I wasn't immediately sure what the list I was spouting was from.

"'Victoria Dew, Sixty-Eight Sycamore Street, Columbus, Ohio. Code Name: the Combustress. ID three-one-one-zero-nine-seven-six-five-four. Powers: Fire creation and control. Origin: Born with powers. Weaknesses: Total vacuums, extreme cold, water. Last mission: Wildfire control in—'"

That's when Dr. Chrysler started clapping. He actually started clapping his hands and dancing around a little.

"I think Doctor C's brain has blown a fuse," Seismyxer announced with a chuckle. I was starting to notice he didn't really distinguish between allies and enemies when it came to mocking people. That's pretty common for bullies . . . even superbullies apparently. That is a fact.

"That is enough, Seismyxer," Necros said with an edge to her voice I hadn't heard before. "Dr. Chrysler, can you stop cavorting long enough to explain why you're so happy?"

"Logan saw the database as it was downloading in MASC HQ. He may have seen the entire thing."

"I saw it too." Seismyxer was doing his snort-laugh

again. "It was scrolling by at warp speed."

"Yes, but you don't have Logan's one-in-a-billion brain. He saw it, *and* he remembers it. Every word. Every detail. Every known individual with superpowers on the planet is inside his head."

Dr. Chrysler unstrapped me from the Houdini chair as he spoke, but Seismyxer seemed confused.

"So we aren't going to wipe the twerp's memory?"

"No, we are not. In fact, there is nothing I wouldn't do to protect his memories right now. Do you understand? Do you *all* understand? Logan is to remain untouched!"

Seismyxer scowled. But then another thought crossed his mind and it was one that I had just had as well.

"Does that mean that the deal with his superfolks is off?"

Necros put her gloved hand on Seismyxer's shoulder. I saw him wince. I guess he didn't like her touching him either.

"They are just two. We now have access to thousands of the most powerful individuals on the planet. This boy is the key to all of them."

I suppose she might have said it to make me feel important, but the way Elena looked at me, I got the feeling it wasn't good news. And when Necros had security drag Elena back to her cell, I knew it for sure.

"Bring in one of our database techs," ordered Dr.

Chrysler. "We will have Logan read back the information from the beginning. It's going to take weeks . . . maybe months, even if we work sixteen hours a day—"

"I don't have to tell you anything," I interrupted; and even though it's not very polite, this time it felt really good. However, the feeling didn't last long.

"No, you don't. Not if you don't wish to."

That was Necros, and she wasn't smiling at all.

"I suppose . . . I will have to make you wish to."

Within seconds, she had her security goons whisk me down the hall to the Containment Unit. There, she walked straight to Gil's and Margie's cells and turned down the dials until both of them were able to focus and see me. Necros spoke, and she didn't sound at all like she did when she was trying to convince them to join her cause.

"I've brought Logan to say goodbye to you."

Gil spoke between the magnetic jolts.

"Then you haven't . . . I mean, he still . . . you haven't wiped his memory yet?"

"No, and we aren't going to."

Gil looked confused, but Margie looked angry. I'd seen that look enough times to recognize it immediately.

"I don't . . ." Gil stammered. "You can't . . . we had a deal!"

"That agreement had to be broken. Logan won't be going anywhere. But one of you will."

Necros turned the dial on Gil's cell back up even higher

than before. The dark matter jolts increased in intensity, disrupting him to the point that I couldn't recognize any part of him. He was screaming, or at least trying to scream. Then she did the same to Margie's cell and I watched her collapse to the floor. Her silver skin was starting to crush like an empty soda can. She was screaming too with whatever air was getting into her lungs. Then Necros turned to me.

"Choose which of your foster parents is going to die right now, Logan. Answer quickly and I'll make the death just as quick. All I have to do is turn one of their dials all the way up."

There was no time for listing possibilities.

Unless Necros was bluffing, all paths led to either Gil or Margie dying. There was no variable or loophole I could find. There was only one option.

"I'll tell you everything."

Necros let Gil and Margie scream for another moment before answering.

"Yes, you will."

5:55 A.M.
SATURDAY, OCTOBER 9

When you and I finally meet for the first time, I would not be surprised if we stay up all night talking and catching up—just for fun.

But staying up all night reciting a database to a guy typing at a keyboard while another person stands behind you with a plasma rifle . . . there is nothing fun about that. That is a fact.

After eight hours of reciting names and addresses, they dragged me back to my cell and locked me in again. All I wanted to do was sleep. But before that could happen, I had to explain what I'd been doing to Gdula and Elena. They were both very concerned, but they were not concerned about the same things.

"Logan, are you okay? Did they hurt you? Where have you been all this time?"

That was Elena from her cell, her hands gripping the bars.

"The girl told me about you memorizing the database. How much did you tell them?"

That was the colonel, standing about three feet behind me, his arms folded.

I ignored Gdula and told Elena what Necros did to Gil and Margie when I refused to help.

"That's inhumane! Logan . . . I'm so sorry!"

Elena seemed even more upset about it than I was, but we couldn't really talk because the man in maroon kept interrupting.

"There are casualties in every war, soldier. You may think you saved your new *mommy and daddy*, but as soon as Necros gets what she needs from you, she will kill them. Then she'll kill you, your friend over there, and me too. You ever think of that?"

I knew there was no way I could trust Necros to keep her word, so of course I had thought of that.

"Of course I've thought of that. But by agreeing to help them, I bought myself—and all of us—some time to come up with a plan."

At that point, Colonel Gdula openly guffawed at me. There was no other way to describe it.

"A plan? Seriously? You're going to come up with a plan to defeat the single most dangerous supervillain on the planet, her quake-making henchman, and the world's smartest expert on superpowers? Why not just whip up some world peace while you're at it?"

"You're an awful person, you know that?"

That was Elena, spitting out her words as her fingers tightened around the bars of her cell, her knuckles showing white. But the colonel stayed focused on me.

"You are no hero, kid. I've worked with all the big ones: the Fantastic Four, the X-Men, Wonder Woman . . . you name 'em. I can tell who's the real deal and believe me when I say *you* don't have what it takes. You're an orphan with a DVR for a brain and a bleeding heart! All you're going to do is give her exactly what she wants—unless you're willing to prove me wrong and do something truly heroic."

Gdula wasn't guffawing anymore. Instead, he was fishing around in a hidden pocket on the inside of his fatigues. When his hand emerged, he was holding a small pill.

"This is cyanide. I'd planned to take it if they were close to breaking me, but right now, you need it more than I do. You know what cyanide does, don't you, Logan?"

Of course, I knew.

"According to the CDC emergency preparedness website, cyanide prevents the cells of the body from using oxygen. When this happens, the cells die. Then the person who took the cyanide dies. Cyanide is more harmful to the heart and brain than to other organs because the heart and brain use a lot of oxygen."

"It was a yes or no question, kid. The point is . . . there's only one pill, and we both know which one of us needs to take it."

"Are you crazy?"

That was Elena again, shouting from her cell. "You want Logan to kill himself? He's twelve years old."

"I'd faked my birth certificate and tried to join the Marines twice by his age," Gdula said with a sniff, like he was proud of falsifying official documents, which is a felony. Then he handed the pill to me. "It's up to you now. But if you aren't going to do the right thing, give it back. Because if you're going to open up that oversized melon of yours and give Necros the very information I've spent half of my life keeping secret, I don't want to hang around to see what she does with it."

I rolled the pill between my fingers for a moment. Now, to be clear, I was *not* considering swallowing it. I knew that it would take weeks of dictation to get every-thing into the computers. That meant Gil and Margie and Elena would be safe until then. I was willing to risk world domination to give them that extra time. That was sur-prising, because it doesn't entirely make logical sense and I didn't know I felt that way until I actually felt that way.

I swear, I was just looking at the cyanide pill . . . but apparently, Elena didn't get that.

"Logan, no!"

And then she did something that I would've assumed

was impossible until I saw her do it. She jumped up, grabbing a pipe running across the ceiling of her cell, which was at least fifteen feet off the floor. Then she swung herself over to the very top of one of the cell's bars where it almost touched the rock ceiling, braced her feet on either side, and bent the bar with all her might. I mean she literally pulled the metal away from the ceiling with her hands until there was a one-foot gap at the very top, which she slipped through in one clean move. She even did a backflip on the way down and landed like an Olympic gymnast in the hall between our cells.

"Holy crud! How the heck did you do that?" I asked, except I didn't say "crud" or "heck." I sometimes curse. That is a fact. But as your big brother, I don't want to be the one teaching you those words.

Elena hit the release button on our cell door and then grabbed the pill out of my hand and threw it into the toilet. Then she gave me a look like she was mad for a second before giving me a hug that was so tight I think I heard a couple of my ribs pop.

"Don't you ever scare me like that again."

"You're one of them!" bellowed Gdula as he crossed his arms like he'd invented the gesture. "At least a level-two superhuman for strength and agility in only your teenybopper years."

"My *teenybopper* years? You are such a . . ." Elena shook her head and refocused on me. "We can talk about my super stuff later. Right now, we need an escape plan. What do you got?"

"Don't ask him," interrupted the colonel again. "I'm the ranking officer here. Here's the plan. You, Wonder Chica, press up against the wall by the door. I'll make a commotion. When the guards show up, you use your L-2 muscles to incapacitate them . . . if that involves lethal force, so be it. I'll commandeer their weapons and . . ."

Elena got even more upset. I could tell because she started yelling at Colonel Gdula, and if my eyes weren't deceiving me from having been open too long, her skin kinda started to glow.

"First of all, don't ever call me *Wonder Chica* again, understood? And second, I'm not going to kill anyone! What's wrong with you? Cyanide pills. Lethal force. Why is your first option always killing someone?"

"Because I'm not playing games. I'm trying win a war to protect humanity!" Colonel Gdula stiffened and jutted out his chin. "And as soon as you're trained and out on the front lines, you'll realize this is how war works."

Elena shook her head again. I think she was either disgusted or had something stuck in her hair. I'm pretty sure it was the first thing.

"Logan, please tell me you've got a better plan."

I actually did.

"I actually do, and I don't think it requires killing anyone. At least I hope it doesn't."

Colonel Gdula started spouting regulations and his credentials and peppering it all with colorful metaphors featuring some words I had never read in any dictionaries.

"Your plan," Elena asked over Gdula's ranting. "How does it start?"

"Well, the first thing involves getting him to stop talking for at least fifteen minutes . . ."

I'm pretty sure I saw a smile flash across Elena's face, but I can't be sure because she moved so fast. And before I could finish the sentence, her right arm streaked out and delivered a crisp, perfect cross to the colonel's chin.

Mid-bluster, Gdula's eyes rolled back in his head and he crumpled into a big pile of burgundy camo on the floor.

"You could have caught him, you know?" I pointed out to Elena.

"I know. So what's next?"

"You're going to have to promise to do exactly what I say . . . and to memorize a really long number. The first part is going to be hard because we're going to have to split up, which I know you're not a big fan of. The second part is going to be hard because memorizing numbers is difficult when you don't have an eidetic memory. But if you trust me . . . there is up to a thirteen percent chance we both get out of here alive."

Elena looked at me for a second.

"We need to work on your pep talks . . . but let's do it."

6:22 A.M.
SATURDAY, OCTOBER 9

My entire life, I've had people telling me I should be quieter, say less, and try not to attract attention. They said it would help me get adopted, or maybe get along better in school. I never once thought that being loud and obnoxious might actually save my life.

Maybe that's why it felt so good to bang on the bars and yell until the security guards showed up. Elena had tucked the unconscious colonel into the lower bunk in our cell so it looked like he was sleeping, then locked us back in and returned to her cell.

"I can't stay here," I explained to my captors in whispered tones. "I need to speak to Dr. Chrysler."

For a moment, the guards seemed ready to turn and

leave me in the cell, so I had to do more convincing.

"Listen, when you guys find me dead in a few hours, you're the ones who'll have to explain to Necros why you didn't get me out while you had the chance."

I watched the guards exchange a worried look. I assumed neither wanted to be the guy who had to explain anything unpleasant to Necros, so they unlocked the cell and pulled me out. As I headed out the door, I threw a look back at Elena and saw her wink at me.

I tried to wink back, but I think I might've just blinked. I'm still not entirely sure how to execute a good wink or even why it's cooler to do it with just one eye.

Necros and Dr. Chrysler appeared surprised when I returned to the room they were in. Seismyxer was nowhere to be seen, which was good news. One less supervillain to deal with.

"He said he needed to talk to you, Mistress Necros," grunted one of the security goons. "He was talking about being dead if we didn't bring him to you."

Necros crossed her arms and drummed her fingers on her biceps impatiently. Dr. Chrysler spoke to speed things up. "What's this all about, Logan?"

"You put me back in a cell with Colonel Gdula. You know he'd rather see me dead than let me tell you what I know."

I'm terrible at lying, but as you can see I did not lie

even once. The biggest mistake liars make is thinking they need to make up everything. But from what I've read, the best lies are ones where everything you say is true, and you just leave out the parts that don't help. That is a fact.

"I'll be safer here, at least until you figure out somewhere else to keep me."

Necros was still suspicious. I guess you don't become the most powerful supervillainess in the world without a healthy skepticism. "When you went in, was the colonel threatening Logan?" she asked the security guards.

"No, mistress," they both answered crisply. "He appeared to be asleep."

"I'm sure he did appear that way."

That was me, still not lying. "But there was no way I was going to sleep in there with him around. Ask Dr. Chrysler. He knows what Colonel Gdula is capable of."

Necros turned her gaze to Dr. Chrysler who nodded solemnly. "He is utterly mission focused . . . plus he doesn't like Logan very much."

She considered the new information for a beat and then had Dr. Chrysler summon someone to do more data entry as they sat me down in the same chair I'd been in all night.

"We'll arrange another secure sleeping space for you, though it may take an hour or so." Dr. Chrysler assured me. "In the meantime, please continue where you left off."

On cue, I started rattling off the information in the

database. But I kept sneaking looks at the clock, hoping Elena's part of the plan was on schedule.

"Can I get up and walk around?" I asked as casually as I could after a few minutes, but it still drew raised eyebrows.

"Why?" Necros asked.

Once again, I had the opportunity to tell a total lie, but told a partial truth instead.

"I was in this chair for about eight hours last night. The Mayo Clinic has linked sitting too long to obesity, high blood pressure, increased risk of death from cardiovascular disease . . . and besides, my butt hurts."

Everyone in the room seemed to accept that immediately. I'm sure many of their butts hurt too from spending a night sitting and listening to me.

Dr. Chrysler sighed. "Go ahead. Just don't touch anything."

So I got up, stretched my legs, and started wandering in little circles around the workstation as the data entry guy kept typing. Dr. Chrysler looked over his shoulder, checking the work. They were both yawning at regular intervals. The rest of the technicians and security guards appeared to be pretty tired too, which was just what I'd hoped.

The only one in the room who seemed to be fully alert was Necros. She watched me pace the whole time, though she said nothing as my little circles got a little wider. She did, however, notice that I kept looking up at the clock. In fact, at one point, she turned to look at the clock too. The ironic thing was, her turning to look at the clock was exactly what I was waiting for.

I made my move. But I didn't run for the door. In fact, I did the opposite. I sprinted away from the door, sat myself down in the nearest Houdini chair, and strapped the headpiece onto my skull before anyone could reach me. Then I spoke in the clearest voice I could muster.

"I would like to renegotiate our agreement!"

6:39 A.M.
SATURDAY, OCTOBER 9

I can tell you that in my life I've freaked out a lot of people. I've freaked out other orphans and entire classrooms and countless potential foster parents. I might have already freaked you out. The thing is, I never did it on purpose before.

But with my finger hovering over a button that would erase at least a month of my memory and possibly a whole lot more, I watched as an entire supervillain organization freaked out all around me . . . just like I planned. Dr. Chrysler slammed a button on the wall, and suddenly there were flashing lights and sirens going off everywhere.

I had expected it, but it was still really loud and I had to fight the urge to cover my ears in order to keep my hand near the control panel.

Within seconds, the room filled with more security goons and then Seismyxer barged in too.

"What the hell is going on? Where's the threat? All I see is the kid."

"The *kid* is the threat, you dolt!" Dr. Chrysler was very agitated.

"Is that why you put him in the chair?" Seismyxer asked. It was a fair question.

"*We* didn't put him in the chair. He put himself in there."

"I'm confused," Seismyxer admitted.

That's when I finally spoke up again, now that I had just about every security commando and supervillain in the whole secret base listening.

"Free Gil, Margie, Elena, and all the other captive superheroes immediately, or else I will erase my own mind and you'll never get your hands on the MASC database."

Everyone in the room looked at each other for a moment. It is possible they'd never seen someone hold himself hostage before.

"You're bluffing, Logan." That was Dr. Chrysler. "You know that if you press that button, you'll be useless to us. Necros will be forced to eliminate your foster parents, your friend, and then you."

"I don't know that at all, actually. Once I'm of no use to you, she might decide to go back to trying to turn Gil and Margie. If that's the case, keeping me and Elena alive would help. But let's say I'm wrong and she does decide to kill us all. Thing is, I have a feeling that's the plan once you get everything out of my head anyway. So if that's the case, I don't have anything to lose . . . but you lose everything I've got up here." I tapped the side of my head. "And at least I get to make it a lot harder for you to take over the planet. So there's that."

Dr. Chrysler raised both eyebrows and looked a little bit impressed (or else a little gassy) as he turned to Necros.

"He really has thought it through."

She nodded and I kept talking.

"Freeing them and keeping me is your best chance of getting what you want. Once you have access to all the superhumans on the planet, letting a few go today won't matter all that much."

For a few beats, it seemed like Necros and Dr. Chrysler were considering it. But there was one person in the room who was unencumbered by deep thought.

"I have another idea."

That was Seismyxer. All attention turned to him, including mine. I watched him closely, my finger hovering over the Houdini chair's control panel. But he never came toward me. In fact, he was slowly backing up.

"Why don't we slow everything down? We're all tired. Why don't you just cool out in that chair . . . I'll lean up against this wall. . . ."

As he spoke, Seismyxer did just that. He casually leaned up against the wall with his hands behind him as if he was relaxing. Of course . . . he wasn't. Suddenly, the wallboard behind him split like a miniature version of the way the ground had split that day at the Promenade. But instead of cracking an entire city block, this rupture was just big enough to split a power outlet at the base of the wall in two. That was an important detail, because my Houdini chair was plugged into that outlet.

The chair's lights and dials went dead.

"A one-in-a-billion brain? Hah! Betcha wish the chair was working now, because a memory wipe is the only way you'll ever forget you got outsmarted by me!"

Seismyxer snorted as he laughed. Why can't bullies ever laugh like normal people? I've never heard a single bully ever laugh through their mouth. That is a fact.

Anyway . . . I just sat there. Apparently, I also smiled, because Seismyxer stopped guffawing for a second.

"What are you smiling at?"

I didn't answer. Instead, Necros did it for me.

"He's smiling because he knows something you don't. He never intended to erase his own memory. Isn't that right, Logan?"

For a good long beat, Seismyxer looked at Necros. Then his face changed into something even I could recognize as pure, undiluted hatred. His hands started glowing and the ground under his feet started to warp like ripples on a pond as a deep rumbling rose up to drown out the sirens.

"You were bluffing?!"

"No, I wasn't, I swear!" I shook my head. He must have believed me because the rumbling and glowing subsided for a moment. "I was stalling. There's a difference."

That's when the walls at the far end of the room exploded in a shower of metal, glass, and dust, to reveal Gil, Margie, and three more superheroes standing where the door used to be.

6:41 A.M.
SATURDAY, OCTOBER 9

If you're thinking that that your big brother was really lucky that all the good guys showed up just as Seismyxer was about to send me tumbling into the core of the earth, you'd be correct. But it's important that you know your big brother wasn't *just* lucky.

I had planned everything down to the minute with Elena. I knew exactly when she was going to sneak out of the cell. I knew when to strap myself into the Houdini chair so that someone would hit the alarm. I knew that would allow Elena to free Gil, Margie, and the others without a ton of attention. And most of all, I knew that if Necros's top enforcer, Seismyxer, was paying attention to me, then five recently freed superheroes could get to me in a matter of minutes while Elena found a way to escape and get help.

So, yes, I was lucky. But I knew I was going to be lucky, so I think that also counts as being smart.

Of course, I had no time to gloat then. I was too busy dodging explosions and volcanic fissures while trying to survive being caught in the middle of a superhuman battle royal.

I'd hopped off the Houdini chair moments before Seismyxer threw a force wave that shattered the entire frame. I'm not certain, but I'd swear he had a grin on his sweaty face as he lined me up for another blast. Just before he could unleash it, TideStrider tackled Seismyxer from behind and called out, "Quarry Lord . . . now!"

Quarry Lord's granite-colored hands swelled to the size of boulders, and he rained blows down on Seismyxer. But Seismyxer was unharmed despite the punishment. The special bands on his wrists seemed to be absorbing a lot of the force. Quarry Lord paused in what looked like confusion, and Seismyxer took the moment to roar and then fire a seismic pulse that catapulted Quarry Lord into TideStrider, flinging them both thirty feet away.

Meanwhile, commandos flooded into the room through the newly created hole in the wall. Margie tossed the gun-toting soldiers aside with a flick of the wrist as their plasma blasts glanced off her metal skin. Gil helped her out by melting their rifles as they aimed them.

On the other side of the room, FemmeFlorance had wrapped an entire squad in the long tendrils that sprang out of her hands. The vines shot out like mini missiles from her fingers, and they tightened around the bad guys, pinning their arms by their sides. It was so cool. She even took a second to wink at me from across the room once. I took that to mean "good job," but maybe she just had something in her eye. There was a lot of dust in the air.

My main goal was to stay out of the fight as much as possible. However, I noticed I wasn't the only one not fighting. At the far end of the room, Dr. Chrysler and Necros were watching the battle unfold. He looked nervous, but Necros didn't appear at all concerned. In fact, she might have even been bored, but her eyebrow raised when she noticed me staring at her. She mouthed an order to a commando nearby and the soldier wove through the battle in my direction. I looked around frantically for an escape route, but there was nowhere to go. Blasts and bricks were flying everywhere.

The soldier got right up into my face, smirked, and said, "We can do this the hard way or we can do it thuuuuuuuuuuuuuh—"

He slumped to the floor mid threat and standing behind him was Elena, holding a wrench like a battle club in her right fist. I was really happy to see her, but I was also confused.

"The plan was for you to get back to the surface and call for help!"

Elena smirked. "You never said I had to stay up there once I did it."

Elena spun on her heel and launched herself at the nearest commando, wrestling the rifle away from him and breaking it over her knee.

Then there was a violent rumble behind me, and I turned just in time to see Seismyxer fire another blast of energy and knock TideStrider and Quarry Lord off their feet again.

Quarry Lord's head slammed into the wall and he crumpled to the floor. TideStrider tried to recover. He groped around the room as if he was looking for anything that would help. Seismyxer started striding toward him, a shoulder-high wave of seismic energy trailing him like an extralong cape of destruction. "Time to die!" I realized that I couldn't do anything myself, but I got an idea.

"Gil! The pipes!"

Gil understood right away, and in a blink, he flashed upward and ruptured the nearest pipe. The nastiest-smelling sewage you could ever imagine spewed all over the floor. It was ultra-disgusting. That is a fact. But apparently TideStrider could control it because he sent a pulsing stream of the stuff straight at Seismyxer. The stink water didn't hurt him, but it slowed him down enough for the moment.

Through the chaos, I saw Dr. Chrysler motioning to Necros, pleading with her to leave with him. But I wasn't the only one who noticed she might get away. FemmeFlorance saw where Necros and Dr. Chrysler were headed and advanced on them. When Necros's personal guards stepped up to block FemmeFlorance's path, she breathed out a fragrant fog that swirled around her. As soon as the guards got close, they fell to the floor, unconscious. In the chaos, Necros and Dr. Chrysler tried to retreat out of the room.

FemmeFlorance was determined to not let that happen. She sent her finger vines toward them and one wrapped around Dr. Chrysler, tripping him to the ground. But Necros kept her feet, and when the vines wrapped around her upper arm and started to pull, Necros slipped a hand out of a glove and touched one of the strands of ivy.

A gray sickness radiated out, coursing down the stalks into FemmeFlorance's wrists. It infected her arms and hands, then her chest, and then up her neck to her head. It looked like what happens to a strawberry when it rots—but in fast-forward. FemmeFlorance's hair wilted and her fingernails browned and curled. I watched as her mouth twisted into a scream that never made it out. In agony,

she turned her head toward me. I watched her eyes, those impossibly green eyes I noticed that first day with Gil and Margie . . . I watched them turn gray.

The strange thing was, I didn't think about the fact that a hero had just died. All I could think about was that three weeks earlier, I had met her, and she had been nice to me. She had invited me back for another tour of her gardens—and now that was never going to happen.

When I was finally able to look away, I turned to Necros. If it's possible, she looked even more beautiful than she had just moments before. I remembered what Dr. Chrysler had said about her ability to take and store a person's life force to make her stronger. It was terrifying. I had just watched a person die for the first time in my life, but all I could think about was how much more alive Necros was. And then Dr. Chrysler stumbled back to his feet, stepping out of the wilted vine around his ankle. He carefully tugged at Necros's sleeve and pulled her toward the door.

I spun around to see how the other heroes were doing. Everyone had their hands full. The only superhero who saw what Necros did to FemmeFlorance was Margie, whose silver skin was radiating rage.

Necros!

I heard Margie's voice booming in my head. Apparently so did everyone else because there was a pause in the fighting.

Necros looked back over her shoulder as Margie thundered toward her. She looked unstoppable—even more impressive than in the Quicksilver Siren comic books.

Of course, none of that mattered. I knew if she reached Necros, she would die too. Maybe the sickness would look different radiating through her silver skin. Maybe her alien biology would let her put up more of a fight. But I had no doubt that if Margie reached Necros and touched her, she'd die just the same, and so I called out to her as loud as I could.

"Mom! Stop!"

6:44 A.M.
SATURDAY, OCTOBER 9

This might be a weird time to pause my story, but I want you to know that I had meant to yell, "*Margie!* Stop!" I don't honestly know why I said "Mom" instead. I've thought about it quite a bit, and there are really only two possibilities:

1. Because I needed her to stop right away and I knew using that word would do it.
2. Because that's how I thought of her in that moment.

It's one of the strange things about my memory. I can recall every word and every detail, but emotions don't always get remembered exactly right. They seem to change over time. That's why emotions and facts aren't the same thing.

I don't know if you grew up with our mother or not. If you didn't, it probably doesn't matter. If you did, you might not like the fact that I called Margie "Mom" and I am sorry if it makes you upset. But I'm not sorry I said it. Margie stopped in her tracks and turned to me, and for a moment, it felt like the battle was over.

Of course, it wasn't—not at all, in fact.

Gil took out the last few commandos in the room, while Seismyxer knocked TideStrider back one more time with a double-fisted wave of power. In the distance, Necros frowned, then turned and stepped through the hole in the wall while Dr. Chrysler scrambled around behind, rousing a few of Necros's elite guards from FemmeFlorance's fog.

"Get up! Get up, you fools! Execute Escape Plan Gamma. Now!"

Margie was still looking at me, her silver skin morphing back to flesh color. She hadn't noticed Necros and Dr. Chrysler getting away yet. But Elena must have seen it all because she went bounding toward the hole in the wall to intercept Dr. Chrysler. The elite guards turned to face her, and Elena squared off against them, fists up and ready for a fight. She landed a right hook that put one of the soldiers on his butt and then spun around to kick the next one in the gut. The third guard threw an elbow that caught Elena just above her cheek and then went to whip out a pistol, but by the time he had it up, Elena had spun behind him and put him in a wrestling hold. They were no match for her.

But then I saw a bright flash, and when my eyes adjusted, Elena was on the floor, out cold. I was totally confused, until I saw Dr. Chrysler standing a few feet away from her, holding the same device they'd used to knock us out in the Seismological Lab.

"Take her!" he ordered the guards. "She may be valuable."

One of the guards slung Elena over his shoulder and they all headed for the exit as I pointed and yelled.

"They're taking Elena!"

Margie's head whipped around and she instantly saw the situation. She took one step toward the hole in the wall and I started to follow. But all of a sudden, a crazy-strong, really smelly arm wrapped around me, crushing the air out of my lungs.

It was Seismyxer, covered in sweat and dust and stinking from all the sewage from the pipe.

"Glad I didn't kill you after all, kid. You're my ticket out of here."

And just like that, I was a hostage again.

I did not enjoy it.

The room was in shambles. There were dozens of commandos out cold. In addition to FemmeFlorance's lifeless body, Quarry Lord wasn't moving at all either. That left Gil, Margie, and TideStrider against Seismyxer. He clearly didn't like those odds, so he put me in a headlock under his disgusting armpit, forcing my head down toward the floor, and started backing up toward the far door.

"Stay back or I'll send a fault line through the kid's spine! Get it?"

I didn't think there was much to get. It wasn't metaphorical. Seismyxer grunted and pulled me along with him.

You want to let him go. . . . You're done fighting.

Margie's telepathy echoed through my brain, even though I knew this time I wasn't her intended audience.

"Your freak-o charms ain't working on me, mama bear." Seismyxer snorted and tapped at his headband. "So back off or the kid is toast!"

Seismyxer shuffled backward across the room, holding me close.

"Don't try anything stupid."

He was actually talking to the heroes and not to me. That was good, because I was definitely thinking about trying something stupid.

I knew that Gil and Margie wouldn't risk an attack as long as I was in danger. So even though I was easily the least powerful person in the room, I realized this time I had to save myself.

The options started flying through my head. There

were no escape routes except the one Seismyxer was steering me toward. The only thing between the door and us was the one remaining Houdini chair; and I noticed that, unlike the one Seismyxer had destroyed, it was plugged into a working outlet, and the touch screen display was still lit up.

There's one thing I have learned from being bullied in half a dozen schools; if someone's walking backward and you stick out your leg behind them, they'll trip every time. It was all geometry and physics—two things I happened to be quite good at.

I noticed that when Seismyxer moved he'd snort first and step with his right foot. Then he'd tell the heroes to stay back and insult one of them before stepping back with his left. Snort, step right. "Stay back, little Miss Silver Skin!" Step left. Snort, step right. "I'll kill him, you pencil neck. . . ."

When he stepped back with his left, my foot was waiting right behind him.

It all happened really fast, but it kinda felt like slow motion too. Of course, that's just my memory slowing it down. I know that from reading the 2007 study "Does Time Really Slow Down during a Frightening Event?" by Chess Stetson, Matthew P. Fiesta, and David M. Eagleman.

First, Seismyxer went tumbling backward and landed

half in, half out of the Houdini chair. His leg kinda draped over one of the armrests like a teenager watching a movie. Then he yelled out, "What the fudge?!" so loudly that the bolts in the ceiling rattled.

(And of course, he didn't say "fudge." And I didn't come up with the idea of substituting the word *fudge* for the bad word on my own. It's from the forty-one-minute mark in the movie *A Christmas Story*.)

Anyway . . . the whole room was undulating underneath everyone's feet. The floor rippled out from where Seismyxer had fallen. But before I lost my footing, I slapped the headpiece on his head and grabbed on to the touch screen unit attached to the chair.

There were two sliding scales on the controls. One said Intensity and another said Duration. I hit the plus button on both as many times as I could before I was shaken loose, and then I pressed the flashing red Erase button just before I lost my grip.

I expected there to be a flash of light or a zap of some sorts. Instead, the Houdini chair just started humming like a microwave heating up a burrito—and as soon as it did, the floor stopped rippling.

I turned to look around and suddenly Gil was by my side.

"Logan . . . you are . . . that was . . . amazing! Are you okay?"

Logically, I knew he was asking about whether I was injured. But I didn't answer that question.

"They took Elena."

Gil seemed surprised and confused for a second, but then he glanced over to Margie and TideStrider and the look on his face changed. When he spoke, he didn't stutter or pun at all.

"Come on. We're getting her back."

6:59 A.M.
SATURDAY, OCTOBER 9

In a blink, Gil was out in the hallway, looking in both directions for any trace of where Necros and Dr. Chrysler might have taken Elena. Margie and I started after him, but then TideStrider spoke up.

"Luther's in really bad shape. We can't just leave him here."

Margie paused and looked down at Quarry Lord, lying on the ground. Then she glanced off to Gil in the hall. "Maybe we should stay until backup arrives . . . or split up? Gil could follow them. . . ."

"But what does that mean for Elena?" I asked urgently because it was genuinely urgent.

With the exception of during meal prep, I had never seen Margie so at a loss for what to do. But TideStrider gave her a nod as he knelt down next to the fallen hero.

"I'll stay here with Quarry Lord and keep an eye on Seismyxer too. You all go and make sure Necros pays for what she did to him . . . and Genevieve. Go."

Margie nodded, then took my hand. We hurried over to Gil.

"Any idea which way they went?"

Margie looked toward one end of the smoke- and dust-filled hall and then toward the other before looking down at me.

"Logan, you've probably seen more of this place than we have at this point. What do you think?"

I thought for a second.

"Dr. Chrysler mentioned 'Escape Plan Gamma,' which means they're heading out. I didn't see anything at all that looked like an exit or an escape pod when Dr. Chrysler was showing me around. But he also never took me down this hall to the left, so by process of elimination . . ."

Gil nodded. "We go left. Let's do this."

He was gone in a literal flash. I ran alongside Margie down the hall, doing my best to keep up with her despite my legs being much shorter and far less powerful or cooperative than hers.

A few times, we heard something up ahead through

the smoke and haze, like a shout and then a muffled impact. Each time, about ten seconds later, we found a slumped-over commando lying in the hall. Gil was clearing the way for us.

Finally, after a few hundred yards of running, which is the most running I've ever done (and the most I hope to ever have to do!), we found Gil waiting by a mostly closed door, his hand up. It's possible he was getting ready to wave hello, but it seemed more likely he wanted us to stop.

"I think this is Necros's chambers. Stay ready."

I held my breath as Gil eased the door open. That was really the most I could do to stay ready.

Inside was a room that was totally different from every other room in the underground lair. For one thing, it was decorated with all kinds of art. There were pieces that looked like they were from ancient Egypt and others that looked totally modern. Also, there was a very fancy bed, a sitting area with couches, and a desk that had just been emptied. All its drawers were hanging open, and a clump of blackened paper had been burned in a wastebasket.

"We missed them. Do you think they doubled back?"

That was Margie, looking over her shoulder at the door we came through. But Gil moved farther into the room, through the haze of smoke and dust that filled the air. After a beat, Gil turned his right hand into a focused beam of bright light and held it still. I could see the smoke was drafting toward the back corner of the room. Gil saw it too.

"There's an air current. It has to lead to a way out."

Gil followed the flowing smoke to a wall panel. He gave the wall a light push. Suddenly, the panel slid aside, revealing a hidden door. But before Gil could go through, Margie stepped up and a silver ripple passed over her entire body as her skin went fully metallic. "Watch my back in case this is a trap."

Gil nodded and Margie shoved open the door and started running up the long flight of stairs she found beyond. I saw her take the steps four at a time until she was at the top, at least fifty feet up, where she paused at another door.

"It's solid steel, with a keypad!" Margie called down to us from above. "Logan, any chance you memorized any key codes while you've been here?"

"No, but according to a Rutgers University study in 2018, the memorability of a password is actually based on—"

Before I could continue, Margie sighed a little, reared back, and threw her shoulder into the metal, blowing the door completely off its reinforced hinges.

Early morning daylight streamed into the stairway as Margie took a second to take in the scene.

"Gil!"

With Margie's voice still hanging the air, I felt Gil scoop me up and rocket both of us to the top of the stairs.

When we emerged from the door, it was like something out of a *Transformers* movie. We were standing in the doorway of what looked like a maintenance shed at the end of Caltech's main quad. The sun was just rising to our right, and the empty quad was mostly shadows, but about a hundred yards away there was a round, central building with a sign that read "Beckman Auditorium." As I watched, I think with equal parts curiosity and fear, the walls started falling away one by one, revealing ten-foot-tall rocket engines on every side. The auditorium was turning into a flying saucer.

Standing in an open portal on the edge of the top disc was Necros. She was holding Elena by the neck with a gloved hand, dangling my unconscious best friend over the edge like she weighed nothing. Necros's other hand, however, was bare and she had it poised just inches from Elena's throat.

Even I got the message. If Gil or Margie made a move, Elena would be dead.

How fast can you get to her?

That was Margie's telepathic voice, whispering to Gil, though I heard it too.

But before Gil could respond, the rockets roared to life

and a wall of fire exploded out from the center of the quad toward us, engulfing every shrub, tree, and bench in sight in less than a second.

"Logan!"

That was Margie as she threw herself at me and wrapped my entire body in hers like a human cocoon. For a millisecond, I saw the burning rocket fuel wash over us and Gil's silhouette disintegrate in the explosion. Then I felt Margie's muscles tense against the shock wave and hold steady. The edges of my clothes turned to ash and I couldn't help thinking about the last time I felt like I might be burned alive, that day on the Promenade.

I have no idea how long the firestorm actually went on. Long enough for me to recite every winner of the Best Supporting Actress Oscar from 1936 to 1962. I'd just muttered "Patty Duke" when the flames finally died down and Margie let me go. That's when I noticed the sound of the fire alarms going off in all the lab buildings lining the quad . . . at least the ones that were still standing.

A beat later, Gil re-formed next to us.

"Are you both okay?"

I nodded. The fact that I was even able to nod meant it was true.

"Gil, she's getting away!"

Margie was pointing up. The rocket saucer was now hundreds of feet up, rising and starting to gain speed. I

could just make out Necros still standing on the saucer's edge, dangling Elena over the side.

Gil's body flashed and I saw his glowing form beam up toward them, but apparently Necros must have seen it too. She held Elena out . . . and let her go.

Elena's limp body fell away from the saucer and started plummeting toward the smoldering crater where the auditorium used to be.

This is usually where I would start running options through my brain, looking for an ideal solution and calculating outcomes. But that didn't happen. I just grabbed Margie's arm and pleaded.

"Tell Gil to catch her!"

Margie looked at me with what I assume was doubt or confusion.

"But if Necros gets away—"

I interrupted and I was not even a little sorry about it.

"I know. But please . . . please tell him!"

Margie looked at me and in that moment, her silver skin faded back to flesh again. Then, even though her lips never moved, her voice echoed clearly in my head as she called up to Gil.

Save Elena!

I looked up just in time to see Gil's streak of light change course and intercept Elena's fall about ten stories above us. It was a bizarre sight. Every few moments, he'd reappear under her and catch her for just a fraction of second, slowing her fall until she reached the ground in his arms.

Margie and I rushed over to where Gil laid Elena down. Gil lit up the tip of one of his fingers and was opening Elena's eyelids one at a time, shining the light in them like at a doctor's exam.

Neither Margie or Gil was speaking, and I couldn't stand the silence. I bent over Elena's prone body and looked right into Gil's eyes.

"Is she alive? Just tell me! Is she . . ."

That's when Elena suddenly gasped and sat straight up, head-butting me right in the forehead. I fell back on my butt on the ashy ground about ten feet away, my eyes watering. On my back, blinking through the tears (and a possible concussion), I could see a rocket trail disappearing into the sunrise. Necros and Dr. Chrysler had gotten away, and it was definitely my fault . . . but I was just as definitely not sorry.

That . . . is a fact.

7:11 A.M.
SATURDAY, OCTOBER 9

I don't know if you grew up with parents, either our biological ones or if you were an orphan who got adopted. But if you did have parents, maybe you can tell me if what Gil and Margie did next is normal.

With fire alarms blaring throughout the quad and the sounds of sirens getting closer from the roads, Gil picked me up off the ground while Margie put an arm around Elena's waist and they basically carried us back into the storage shed that led down into Necros's lair.

"Elena, we told you to get to safety when you freed us!" Margie said, using her substitute teacher voice. "You were almost . . . I don't even want to say it. You know what almost happened."

"I know, Ms. Morrow . . . I mean Margie."

Gil set me down at the bottom of the stairs and put his hands on his hips.

"And you . . . young man . . . Logan . . . I mean . . . We're supposed to keep *you* safe. You shouldn't even be here. We said stay home . . . and wait . . . and you . . . are supposed to listen . . . to us."

I responded. "I don't often do what I'm supposed to do. You should probably know that about me. Besides, if I had . . . you would both probably be dead."

Gil started to speak, but then paused. And then started to speak again. But it wasn't like his usual stutter.

Finally, he admitted. "You know what? That is a fact."

And then he laughed. So did Elena. Margie even smiled, though I don't think she wanted to.

We quieted down and carefully worked our way back into the lair, not sure if any of Necros's forces were still there. But when we finally returned to the room where TideStrider was watching over Quarry Lord's unconscious body, I noticed something. The Houdini chair was still on, with a totally blank-faced Seismyxer lying there vacantly.

"You didn't shut it down?" Margie asked TideStrider, who looked up with a hard glare. "What if the machine erases something important?"

"I don't care if that creep forgets how to use the bathroom by himself. I wasn't doing anything that might wake him up until you guys got back."

Gil cleared his throat.

"I've never seen anyone in the chair this long. Should I . . . ? I'm . . . I'm gonna shut it off."

While Gil powered down the machine and removed Seismyxer's protective headband and wristbands, TideStrider picked Quarry Lord off the floor.

"He's barely breathing. If we don't get him help right away . . . I don't know."

You might think that heroes always know what to do because that's the way they seem in the comic books, but they don't. They're like regular people in that regard.

Suddenly, there was a sound coming from out in the hall. Actually, lots of sounds: military-style boots pounding the concrete floor in our direction, the sound of plasma rifles being cocked and charged.

TideStrider laid Quarry Lord down on the ground between me and Elena and then joined Gil and Margie, bracing themselves for a new round of battle as they formed a semicircle in front of us. I appreciated it. I was kind of done being the target for the day.

And then the commandos burst through the door, weapons raised. They were all in gray camo, led by Colonel Gdula, who was sporting a newly lit cigar held between his teeth, just above his very swollen jaw.

In that tense moment, I wondered if my decision to have Elena find a phone and call the MASC secret rescue number was the right one. But then, just when I was expecting the next sound I heard to be plasma blasts and explosions again, someone's voice broke the silence.

"Where am I?"

We all turned and saw Seismyxer slowly sitting up in the Houdini chair. He looked utterly bewildered, and he wasn't the only one.

7:24 A.M.
SATURDAY, OCTOBER 9

I have learned that the ability to figure something out, and the ability to explain what you figured out are not the same thing. I am exceedingly good at the first one. But I tend to include too many details when doing the second thing. Like way too many details. Like all the details.

So when the MASC commandos and the superheroes all realized that Seismyxer was awake and apparently unaware of why he was there, I left it to others to explain. But I quickly figured out we had to get the soldiers surrounding Seismyxer to stand down and lower their weapons. The floor kept rumbling every time the brain-wiped bad guy got too tense.

After asking Seismyxer a few questions, it became clear that the Houdini chair had erased about the past ten years of his memory. He still thought he was a college freshman, which meant he had no idea he had any superpowers. That said, he was still a jerk. He just didn't know he was a spectacularly powerful jerk.

When asked about Necros, he thought the name sounded like an energy drink. Then he started talking about how he'd like an energy drink. Finally, upon noticing his costume, he seemed convinced that he had been the victim of a fraternity prank. Colonel Gdula let him keep thinking that as he instructed a small team of MASC guards take him back to his "dorm room."

I put "dorm room" in quotes because I'm fairly certain they actually were going to take him to a MASC detention facility . . . maybe forever.

"You did an excellent job keeping him alive," Gdula growled grudgingly as he stepped toward Gil and Margie.

"Logan's our son. Of course, we kept him alive."

"I meant Seismyxer," Gdula said, shaking his head. "Even without his memory, we may be able to leverage him in some way. Maybe he can be reprogrammed to work for us. If nothing else, he's one less weapon Necros can use."

By this point, a second team from MASC had entered

the room. Mostly medics and scientists. They took Quarry Lord, who was still unconscious, and put him on a cool hoverstretcher as Gdula continued to bark orders.

"Get him topside and medevac him to the nearest medical facility we have. We're low on assets on the West Coast as it is. We need him back on his feet." Finally, he turned his attention to me.

"And now to deal with you."

Gil and Margie closed ranks in front of me. I wasn't worried about him grabbing me or anything, but I didn't mind the protection, especially when TideStrider stood beside my foster parents and Elena stepped up to join them. Gdula shook his head and grimaced.

"You, son, are a bona fide menace; a walking, nonstop-talking, global security breach waiting to happen. In the entire the history of MASC, you may be the single greatest threat to the work we do. Give me one good reason why I shouldn't put you in the Houdini chair until your brain is blanker than a ream of copy paper?"

I wanted to say something clever back to him, but I realized he was right. I am not great at keeping secrets. That is a fact.

Luckily, I wasn't the one who answered him. Elena spoke first.

"Logan is the reason I was able to find and free the heroes in the first place. It was his plan."

"And without his help," TideStrider pointed out, "I'd be on that medevac chopper next to Quarry Lord—or dead like FemmeFlorance."

"He also single-handedly neutralized Seismyxer and kept the database out of Necros's hands."

That was Gil, who didn't stutter or make a pun once. Then Margie spoke.

"And like I said . . . Logan's our son. So you don't get to put him anywhere . . . unless you want three of the last few healthy assets you have in this time zone to become free agents."

I don't think Colonel Gdula liked that last point at all, but he really had no choice.

"So who *does* get to decide what happens to the little son of a . . ." Margie's skin glimmered silver and I think Gdula noticed because he never finished the sentence.

"He does."

That was Gil, and he put an arm on my shoulder. I let him leave it there, and not just because I knew it wasn't actually a human arm.

"And what if I still don't trust him?" Gdula asked.

By this point, several of Gdula's commandos were standing behind him, weapons in hand. Things felt like they were getting tense, but I actually knew the correct answer to his question.

"It takes time and effort to build trust. Someone told me that once . . . sixty-two hours ago. It seems like a lot longer now, though."

Gil and Margie both smiled at me quoting them. Colonel Gdula did not. He gave his cigar one more grind between his teeth and then turned, barking orders to his team to sweep the rest of Necros's facility. TideStrider went with them in case they needed superpowered back up.

"You okay, Logan?"

That was Elena, whose right eye was just about swollen shut by this point.

"Yeah, but your eye looks terrible."

Elena shook her head and smiled. "You really know how to flatter a girl. I'm gonna go see if that medical team has an ice pack. My mom is gonna freak when she sees this shiner." And then she walked across the room, leaving me alone with Gil and Margie.

It was strange because it was the first time in two and a half days we were all together without worrying about being attacked or captured. But I could hardly remember what it was like when I was just a new foster child to two odd people who were keeping something from me.

I mean, I could obviously remember everything. I just couldn't really remember how I'd felt about it. So much had changed.

"Logan." Margie looked at me and smiled, but she still kind of looked sad too. "We meant what we said. It is your decision. Necros knows who you are now. You would probably be safer if you allowed MASC to wipe your memory and relocate you with no ties to us."

Gil held Margie's hand and nodded.

"But they're your memories, Logan . . . your life too. We want you to be with us for as long as you want. Another week . . . a year . . . longer maybe. But more than anything, we want what's best for you, even if that means we . . . we don't get to be your foster parents anymore."

I watched Margie's hand tighten on Gil's. She squeezed so hard I was worried his molecules might disassemble. But then Margie reached out with her other hand.

"Come here."

I stepped forward and took her hand. Luckily, she was gentler with me.

"It's okay, Logan. You just tell us what you want, and we'll respect your decision."

As I've told you, I'm somebody who is used to considering all the possibilities, and there were certainly plenty of variables in play in this case. Multinational secret organizations and foster parents who were living double lives. Beautiful new neighbors who actually liked me and ultrapowerful villains who might want my brain. Eating mediocre meals at ESTO or trying to choke down Margie's alien cuisine. I could go on with this list for pages. But right there in that moment, maybe for only the second time in my life . . . there was only one option that made any sense to me.

5:48 P.M.
SUNDAY, OCTOBER 10

Have you ever noticed that people seem surprised when they leave a place and come back to find it hasn't changed much? Like they think them leaving should have made some massive difference? They always say something like, "It's just as I remembered it." Barnabas Collins said those exact words in episode 212 of the TV show *Dark Shadows*. Maybe you've said it too.

You should know I'm never surprised when someplace is just as I remember it. I remember everything exactly as it was, so I'm more surprised when there's been a big change. That's not to say that people and places don't change. They do.

When I walked into ESTO with my box of comic

books held in front of me, I hadn't been there in three weeks and one day. It was actually the longest I'd been away from ESTO since I moved in at age three. None of my previous placements had lasted more than two weeks. So the fact that nothing had changed didn't surprise me.

There was the same avocado-green paint ready to flake off the common room walls at any moment, the same ancient computer on a desk in the corner, and the same dozen boys who had been there when I'd left in Gil and Margie's rented minivan. Mal was bullying a couple of the younger orphans to give up their seats on the couch, threatening to put a booger in their hair if they didn't move. His right index finger was a knuckle deep in his nostril, so it definitely wasn't an idle threat. Jordan was sitting at the card table, trying to convince Jesus that the Hulk had actually caused global warming. And Ms. Kondrat was tidying up the game shelf, looking only mildly annoyed . . . until she saw me.

"Logan . . . it's . . . you're . . . you've got a box . . . I didn't get a . . . are you? . . . No one informed . . ."

This is just a partial list of partial sentences that tumbled out of Ms. Kondrat. They were interrupted only by short little inhales that made me wonder if she was dealing with a restrictive lung disease. According to Dr. Jonathan Robert Caronia, there are five different classes of these diseases, including pleural, alveolar, interstitial, neuromuscular, and

thoracic cage abnormalities. But I'm pretty sure she was just out of breath because she wasn't expecting me to show back up.

"You weren't expecting me to show back up, were you, Ms. Kondrat?"

"No . . . I mean, yes . . . I mean usually our foster parents call before they . . . where are Mr. Grant and Ms. Morrow? They didn't just drop you off like the Messlers did, did they?"

"Did that really happen, Logan?"

That was Margie, who had just climbed the steps into the common room with Gil.

"The Messlers didn't even walk me inside. They left me and my stuff on the curb next to the recycling bin."

"I've heard of being *dumped*, but that's a whole new level."

I actually thought Gil's joke was sort of funny, but it was clear Margie didn't. She jabbed Gil in the ribs hard enough for his molecules to scatter.

Ms. Kondrat didn't notice. She was still trying to sort out what was happening.

"So I see you have a box of comics, Logan. Are you . . . ?"

She didn't finish her thought, but she was right. I did have a box with every single comic book I owned.

"I wanted the other boys to have them. I've read them all, and won't be needing them for trading anymore.

Besides, I've decided I'm not so into semifiction."

"What do you mean?"

It was a good question. But for once, I didn't answer with all the information I had. First of all, I knew it would take way too long. Second, I looked to Gil and Margie who were subtly shaking their heads and I understood what they meant.

Ms. Kondrat wasn't my favorite adult ever, but I didn't think she deserved to have her memory wiped, so I kept the details to myself.

"I just mean I've outgrown them."

I handed the box to Ms. Kondrat, who thanked me, and then Gil, Margie, and I headed back out the way we'd come in.

But before I went down the front steps one last time, I looked back. Ms. Kondrat had dropped the box of comics off on the table by the TV and then went to her office and shut the door.

As soon as Ms. Kondrat was out of sight, the boys rushed to the box, grabbing up my old comic books.

And then I left the orphanage for good. I got back into Gil and Margie's minivan, and we drove the same exact route to their house as we had nearly a month before, except this time, I actually knew what to expect, instead of just thinking I did.

When we got back to Kittyhawk Circle, Elena was waiting outside one of her houses—the one on the left. Her hair was hanging kind of down across her face, covering up her black eye.

"It looks like it's healing a bit."

Elena smirked. "Yeah, I promise you I look better than that commando who hit me. Of course, I can't tell my mom that. She still thinks I got elbowed in a pickup game at the park."

"I'm sorry you have to lie. I'm also sorry for almost getting you killed, like, three different times."

"Hey, what are neighbors for, right? Borrow a cup of sugar, ask us to water your plants while you're away, help save the world from a superpowered uprising . . ."

Elena grinned even wider, but I just looked at her. "Gil and Margie don't have any indoor plants."

I waited a second before I smiled. I had made a joke. Elena seemed impressed.

Of course, I knew that we weren't going to be neighbors anymore. MASC was going to give Gil and Margie new secret identities and relocate us one town over, down the hill from Westchester . Elena also told me that MASC had started recruiting her to join their junior program and get superhero training.

"Are you gonna do it?"

"Not sure. I'm more interested in doing some non-superpower training first. You ready for that bike riding lesson? I didn't survive, like, four near-death experiences just so you could move away and ditch me."

"It was only three, actually."

Elena put her hands on her hips. "I'm serious, Logan! You gotta get good enough on this thing so you can ride over and visit me once you move."

And that was all it took to motivate me. I actually wanted to learn to ride a bike for the first time in my life. I put on my helmet and started pedaling . . . and crashed . . . and got back up and tried again. I was still pretty awful at it, but I noticed it didn't feel as scary as it had all the other times.

It's good we aren't planning to move too far away. It's a distance I'll be able to handle once I get a bit more proficient. So I won't have to try and make another friend like Elena, which would be just short of statistically impossible. That is a fact.

Gil and Margie and I have agreed that we won't discuss them adopting me for a little while so we can see how things work out. Between MASC still not being exactly thrilled with me, the threat of Necros seeking revenge, and the fact that I've been told I'm not always the easiest person to live with, we all decided we should start the process over and do it a bit more honestly.

Now that I know who Gil and Margie really are, it makes things easier. I've even decided to try calling them "Mom" and "Dad" sometimes, just to see how it feels. They both seem to really like it. I know that because they both told me so. They said they feel like they are getting to know the real me too, which I'll admit, I don't totally understand. In the past, most of the trouble I've gotten into has come from my inability to be anyone except who I really am.

Gil and Margie also promised me that in our new home, I'll have my own computer so I can keep categorizing the thousands of cat videos that are uploaded every day, and even more importantly, keep looking for you.

That's what I'm going to do. I promise. If anything, this past month has made me realize that just about anything is possible—even finding you.

I'll keep chasing leads until we have a chance to meet once and for all. Because even if I do keep living with Gil and Margie . . . even if they decide to adopt me someday and I decide to let them, you will always be my little sister or brother. You are the missing piece . . . and I'm *really* good at puzzles.

I'll also keep writing to you, just in case. Even though my life has gotten a little more normal in some ways, I'm pretty sure the not-so-normal stuff has only just begun.

But if I can stay alive long enough and keep anyone from pressing the delete button on my memory, I still believe I'll find you someday. And when I do, you can read all of this and know that even though I can't remember you . . . I've never forgotten you either.

That is a fact.

ACKNOWLEDGMENTS

Just like in this book's pages, there truly are heroes all around us. In my case, they're the people who stood by me, urged me on, and kept me sane as I chased the dream of making this book a reality. So I want to thank as many of the special folks as I can now, before they fly off.

Every hero has their origin story, and mine starts with the real Gil and Margie, my parents. With your blood in my veins and your words, "look it up, Shawn" echoing in my ears, how could I have been anything but a writer? I hope you both find favorable aspects of yourselves in your namesakes and know you're my heroes.

I am forever grateful to my agent, Rick Richter (that's gotta be a superhero secret identity name, right?), as well as Caroline Richter and the rest of the team at Aevitas Creative Management. Logan might have languished on the slush pile indefinitely, stuck in the literary version of an orphanage, if Rick hadn't been "smitten" by the voice and the story. Thank you for taking a shot on me, Rick, and for pushing me to make this book better, leaner and cleaner in every way. You always have my back and you faithfully deliver on what you say you can do. It's amazing.

The next member of this league of heroes has to be my editor, David Linker. From our first phone call, we had a shared vision of what this book could be and who it would be for. Along the way, I discovered that however much Logan reminds me of myself, it's actually you, Dave, that can channel Logan's POV. I am so lucky to have had you as a partner in this entire process and I'm humbled by the faith you showed in believing this story was bigger than just one book.

I'd be remiss if I didn't give a huge shout to the rest of the superpowered team at HarperCollins, starting with Carolina Ortiz, who offered invaluable perspective and expertise. The copy-editing prowess of my production editor, Jessica Berg, was truly supernatural and I was constantly blown away by the dedication to detail from her, as well as proofreader supreme Mary Ann Seagren. And I'm in awe of Vaishali Nayak, Jacquelynn Burke, Corina Lupp, and Alison Klapthor because they're the ones who made Logan's story come alive in vibrant color and did the heavy lifting to make sure the world knows about this kid. He's grateful and so am I.

On a personal note, I owe so much to Sue Gilad, Debbie Olshan, and Jen Lutzky, who all read the earliest drafts and gave me the feedback and hope I needed. I was fortunate to have generous and gracious author friends like Antoine Wilson, Adriana Trigiani, and especially Julie Abbot Clark (a true debut-whisperer), who offered encouragement, insights, and support. And I was more than blessed to have friends and fellow fathers, like Jon Glazer and Mike Keohane, who read the book and heard something familiar and true in Logan's voice. I hope I got the important parts right, and if I did, it was also with the help of a thoughtful and thorough sensitivity read from Sarah Pripas.

Before this book even had representation, it was "award winning" thanks to Bridget Hodder and the rest of the Marble-head Festival of the Arts. Winning the prestigious Golden Cod in the summer of 2018 was a turning point for this book.

But the readers I owe the most to are dozens and dozens of students in Mrs. Peters' fifth grade classes at Miller Elementary School in Holliston. Authors dream that their work will end up in the hands and hearts of their intended audience, and you all made my dream come true before the book was ever published. Your feedback, questions, and love for this book inspired huge rewrites and massive confidence.